Pages for You

Sylvia Brownrigg is a novelist and reviewer. She was born in California where she spent much of her childhood before moving to Oxford with her family. She graduated from Yale University with a degree in philosophy. She now lives in London and reviews regularly for the *Times Literary Supplement* and the *Guardian*. She is the author of two previous critically acclaimed works, a short-story collection *Ten Women Who Shook the World* and a novel, *The Metaphysical Touch*.

'An exuberant feat of storytelling that you simply can't help falling for' Leo Walstow, *Glamour*

'A thrillingly intimate book, and just the right read for the feeling–frisky season. Swoonsomely romantic'
Eithne Farry, *Elle Magazine*

'A hauntingly beautiful love develops . . . in this tale either for young readers first discovering who they are and how they love, or for those remembering a rose–coloured past' Booklist, Amazon.com

'She is obviously one of the most exciting new writers of her generation' James Wood

'Language is the real object of infatuation here. An atmosphere gradually forms in which words are as seductive as bodies . . .'
Independent on Sunday

Also by Sylvia Brownrigg

Ten Women Who Shook the World
The Metaphysical Touch

Sylvia Brownrigg

·····················

Pages for You

PICADOR

First published 2001 by Farrar, Straus and Giroux, New York

This edition published 2002 by Picador
an imprint of Pan Macmillan, a division of Macmillan Publishers Limited
Pan Macmillan, 20 New Wharf Road London N1 9RR
Basingstoke and Oxford
Associated companies throughout the world
www.panmacmillan.com

ISBN 978-0-330-48462-6

5 7 9 8 6

A CIP catalogue record for this book is available from
the British Library.

Printed and bound in the UK by
CPI Mackays, Chatham ME5 8TD

Visit **www.picador.com** to read more about all our books and to buy
them. You will also find features, author interviews and news of any author
events, and you can sign up for e-newsletters so that you're always first to hear
about our new releases.

For a friend

PROLOGUE

What would happen if I wrote some pages for you? Each day a page, to show you that I am finding a story, the story of how we might have been together, once. Of how we could be.

We will never be together. *Sweetheart.* I am too brittle, hidden, and snappish, and you are too married. You are altogether too married. For those of us who've never known the state it sails past us like a cruise ship, lamps all on and parties raging, as the water gently or rockily allows you to sweep across it. We wave from our smug or perhaps lonely shores, waiting till the sea-scattered brightness has withdrawn its silvery music, and we're left alone in the dark, on dry land, to carry on with our unfettered midnight explorations.

He's a lovely man, your Jasper, not that I know him. I know of his qualities by how he illuminates you—you can see the light of him all through your body and most particularly your face as you tell tales of your joint adventures: clifftops and forest walks and long, cool, medieval alleys. Forget-me-not seas and the heart-pure beaches beside them, along which you can both sun-stretch silently or speak. Galleries and night strolls, concerts and banquets. Language and travel, and the many ways those twain shall meet. So alive are these narratives on your wantable mouth and in your essential eyes that I can watch them, movies in my quiet head to play when I'm at home, stirring in my empty rooms, waiting for my own ship to come in.

It will come. They'll find room for me somewhere. Someone will cough up an extra berth on some deck or another, or there will be a lucky last-minute cancellation. Who knows, maybe I'll even be given a seat at the captain's table to mingle with all the uniformed fellows and their glorifying wives. No—not the captain's table for me, probably. Probably something more like Table Thirteen, with the insurance agents and medical eccentrics, where I can be fêted as a storyteller—*Really! But how wonderful! Tell us, what kinds of stories?*—and be allowed to sip my sparkling water without causing too much trouble. I'll sit at my table onboard and silently toast you, across the oceans, where you'll be sparkling at yours.

In the meantime, I have treats in store for you. A perfect, pitch-purple aubergine; caramelized fennel; potatoes roasted in rosemary, for remembrance. Coriandered orzo tossed with chicken and okra. Kiwis and tangerines. Cake moist with all the ginger and butter one girl can politely afford, to create something fragrantly spiced and suggestive, a taste to remind you of a late glass of wine and mood-loosened limbs: that question in the eyes, or the stray touch of one's hand on another one's forearm. The never-kissed kiss. The imagination ignited.

Enough. Enough. The taste treats are real, or will be. Now, here are your pages.

PART ONE

The leaves were confettied brightly over the sidewalk as if a parade had just passed, and Flannery did not think she had ever in her life seen such colors. They would get deeper and more heartfelt, she knew, with warm oranges and pomegranate reds, and she could hardly wait for the experience. Like every other sensation, that sight was still before her. But already they were goldenrod and butternut on the ground, and up in the trees (she looked skyward) infinite greens, all the apple and lime and melon flesh she could imagine. They were so beautiful she wanted to eat them or breathe them, take them inside her, make them part of herself. At the very least, she wanted to not ever forget them. She told her memory to hold on to them; there might come a time later when she would need their solace.

She came from a place where autumn meant oncoming dampness and fog, the new drawl of the school year: a plain, dull gravity of shoulders and hope. Nothing like this fierceness of light and the brisk bite of cold on the cheek, which seemed playful, a love nip, rather than a somber slap of warning that winter might come. She was not yet wary of the winters here, having not moved through one. She knew this approaching splendor meant death and decay, the boding of ice-prisoned branches and slippery black streets, but could not make herself feel the grief in it. All this vividness she could read only as exhilaration. Not melancholy.

Flannery abandoned herself to movie clichés of the East she'd learned as a girl in the West. She kicked her tennis-shoed feet through the leaves. She buried her hands in the pockets of her coat, which had a serious weight she was not used to. She knew that this lift of fall glory, which brought her to a shocking peak of happiness—from where, suddenly, she had a complete panoramic view; could see the shape of her future, the blank scope of her forthcoming cities and days—she knew that she would never again reach such a height of pure, sensual pleasure. Never again in her life.

She was seventeen. She had no idea about anything, really. And she was about to meet someone—literally, around the next corner.

Within that person, a new and altogether unsuspected happiness waited.

Around the corner was a diner. *Diner:* even the words were new here, as if she were in another country, which every single minute she felt herself to be. She had grown up with coffee shops, not diners. She had eaten not grinders but subs. She'd never considered, not for a moment, the idea of a jelly omelette.

This diner was called the Yankee Doodle, a cheerful name that belied the cramped gloom of the place. The Yankee Doodle had jelly omelettes on the menu, and Flannery was feeling bold as she sat down. Sure, she could have a toasted bran, corn, or blueberry muffin—it hardly mattered which, they were essentially the same, and she could in anticipation taste the crisp buttered edge of each neat disk—but with the gold splendor still in her spirit from the leaves, she said to the prune-faced waitress who waited, wiry with impatience and sarcastic with accent,

"A jelly omelette, please. And a glass of orange juice."

The waitress nodded, scribbled on her pad, and retreated behind the narrow Formica counter, along which a few jacketed shapes huddled over hot drinks and doughnuts, or hash browns mixed with ketchup-bloodied eggs. To a stooped, white-shirted man whose balding head was all but lost to steam clouds of grease, the waitress instructed with unneeded volume,

"Jelly omelette!"

The phrase, ridiculous when spoken, especially so loudly in the bored voice of the waitress, had a single advantage. It caught the attention of a figure sitting at a table in a near corner, from whom Flannery might otherwise have hidden as she sank back into her familiar state of wrong-footed self-consciousness.

Dressed in black, drinking coffee, smoking a cigarette. Absorbed in a book—until, that is, "Jelly omelette!" broke the concentration. In one of those gifted premonitions, Flannery noticed the reader an instant before "Jelly omelette!" was barked, so that she was directly facing the elegant autumn-shaded head and already wondering keenly what the book might be.

The green eyes looked up in an irritated humor, to see who could possibly be the author of such an order.

Flannery saw the reader's eyes, her cat green eyes, and stopped breathing. Never in her life—not at least since the leaves—had she seen such a heartbreaking color.

To that green glitter of mockery—Flannery's breakfast request was, from an adult, hardly credible—the hungry girl replied with a smile of embarrassment, an apologetic shrug of the shoulders. *I can't help it,* Flannery tried to suggest. *I don't know what I'm doing.* There was no smile in return. The reader's glance-flicker was so brief that Flannery's shoulders were still winced up in their shrug when those eyes turned back to their pages and the serious lips took a deep drag from a cigarette.

Oh. God. Those lips. It was the cigarette that made Flannery notice them, now that the reader's eyes were turned down toward her book. Flannery had nothing to do but watch that mouth smoking, and though she couldn't have said why it was so beautiful or described the thrill of its shape—she was too young to have anything like a vocabulary for such things—she could not stop herself from watching it, shaded a darkish persimmon that left its trace on the cigarette. But the ash was low, Flannery saw, and soon the fine, purposeful fingers were stubbing it out. Flannery looked away quickly, panicked, frightened of further emerald mockery if she was caught staring so unashamedly.

The waitress brought her her orange juice, and Flannery took a great swallow as if it were a shot of vodka. It was fakely sweet and an unlikely color, more like a billboard or paint shade than any real fruit. Its strange flavor made her mouth pucker, and she was relieved that the waitress was soon back with a different taste to replace it: a lightly browned yellow omelette, thrown gracelessly onto a thick white oval plate.

Flannery stared down at it a moment. What had she asked for? What was a jelly omelette, actually? With the side of her fork she tentatively cut into it, a clean slice off the edge. Out of the cut leaked a thick translucent purple, as if she'd hit some alien vein. The purple was, she realized, none other than grape jelly. The purple and yellow textures avoided each other uneasily on the plate. They were not meant for each other: being together did not suit them. Flannery put down her fork and sipped her juice, for courage.

Something made her risk a look at the reader, and she was sure that she saw a telltale dip of the head, as if the woman had just been watching *her*. Emboldened by the idea, Flannery kept her gaze on the now nonsmoking figure, who took a sip of black coffee. And another. She turned the page. She pursed her lips. (Those lips!) She brushed a lick of deep reddish brown hair behind a delicate ear. She sipped her coffee. Her eyes moved to the next page. Flannery abandoned her omelette and watched the woman drink her coffee. Still, she wanted to know: What was the book?

It worked. The reader's concentration wavered, and finally she looked up, one of her eyebrows raised, an ironic expression.

"Don't like your breakfast?" she asked in a sly voice, so that the waitress could hear. Flannery didn't want to come right out and admit it, so she shrugged again, mutely. Idiotically. "You seem," the reader went on, reaching for another cigarette, "to like the look of my coffee, from the way you're staring. Perhaps you should order a cup for yourself, if that's what you want."

That did it. Flannery flushed from the chest up, a full hot plum of humiliation. She looked away, asked for the check, paid it, and fled the Yankee Doodle. Without looking back. Without waiting for her change.

On the street again, her heart was noisy in her ears, from her fast walk and her embarrassment. Not so noisy, though, that it outbeat the internal words of her silent reply.

It wasn't that she *wanted* the coffee, no. That wasn't it. Rather, she wanted to *be* the coffee: she envied the dark drink its chance to taste those lips.

She never should have come here. She did not belong. If Flannery belonged anywhere—which her uneasy skin and awkward, long-legged gait made her doubt—it could not possibly be on these busy old university grounds, in a year that had seasons, alongside such sour-souled people. They were all planning to laugh at her, clearly, every single day, until she finally gave in and went back to the land of computers and eucalyptus, where everyone wanted you—sincerely—to have a nice day.

"Hey, Flannery!" called a thin-coated ally from across the traffic-blurred street. Another westerner, whom Flannery had met on the first day. They lived on the same floor and shared a crowded bathroom. She was called Cheryl, which made Flannery uneasy, but then with a name like Flannery you could not afford to be choosy. "Are you going to that Intro to Criticism class? It starts in ten minutes."

"Another new one? Isn't it a bit late by now?" She already felt she'd been here half a lifetime; it had been two weeks.

"Yeah, but the professor's just gotten back. From *Paris*. Bradley. He's supposed to be great."

There had been so many beginnings, it seemed—when would they end? Still: *Criticism*. It could be what she needed. A weapon. Fight them at their own game. Learn the language of prunes.

"Sure." She fell in step with her half-friend. "Do you think I have time to grab a muffin from the dining hall on the way over?" Her stomach yawned hungrily.

Cheryl checked her watch. "If we hurry," she said. "But didn't I just see you walk out of the Doodle?"

"Of the what? Oh yeah, but—"

"Better watch it," Cheryl teased. "It's early days to be putting on the freshman fifteen, already."

The sunny girl playfully reached out to pat Flannery's stomach. It took all the taut self-restraint Flannery had not to slap her.

The first of any class seemed to be a scuffle of papers and faces, a busy fantasy of the great heft of new knowledge that might soon be gained. Flannery had already signed up for a weighty range of subjects: Intro to Art History; Intro to Revolution: France, Russia, China; Intro to World Fiction; Intro to Animal Behavior. Flannery wondered how she would find time for all these introductions.

Perhaps the blazered, grizzled figure at the sloped bottom of the high-windowed room, who leaned what seemed tipsily into the wooden podium, was indeed great. Flannery could certainly not tell from his introduction to this Introduction. He intoned a litany of words that she did not know but could identify as different weeks on the dense syllabus; he fluently pronounced European names whose printed equivalents she could just pick out on the list of required reading. After he had finished his bewildering garble on the material they might all one day be masters of, he mentioned that there were sections to sign up for—supplementary classes run by graduate students who did the grading, explained Cheryl in a cough-drop whisper, as if Flannery didn't already know it. Sections were taught by Bob or Anne, figures who sat in the classroom's front row, backs to the students, raising their weary graduate arms for identification. How to choose between

Monday Bob or Tuesday Anne? Like so many of her decisions, Flannery made this one blindly. She chose Anne. Tuesday Anne.

"Goody, I'll pick her, too, then," said Cheryl, holding Flannery's arm.

Flannery held her breath. Intro to Criticism. Here we go. *'Goody,'* she practiced quietly, in the privacy of her own thoughts, *is not something that we, as college students, any longer say. It makes you sound like a fifth-grader.*

Maybe she could get the hang of living here, after all. Would the crafting of such retorts be covered in this basic introductory course?

D_{ays} she staggered; but nights she swam free, through the cool waters of her imagination. Her body was relieved in the dark of its shy apologies, and her young hands wandered over her own flesh, as if for the first time. She allowed herself whatever late hours she needed for this discovery, even if it made her sleepy for the next day's Revolution, relying on Coke to power her through the forced labor of note-taking.

How could Flannery be so old and still not know herself? For this seventeen-year-old did feel old. Those private years of intense adolescent reading and music-fueled writing in her journal had made her sure she was full of maturity—of a certain unusual, and in its way impressive, emotional self-assurance. She had an alert awareness of what people were like. She'd talked two of her high-school friends through the loss of their virginity, even as she'd held on easily to her own.

Flannery's assurance did not reach to her sexual self. She and her body were only now beginning to speak to each other. Where had she been, she sometimes wondered, when all the other six- and eight-year-olds were busy playing nurse and doctor, undergoing examinations in the shaded end of the garden? Why hadn't her mother ever discovered her and some little friend fondling each other in the closet, so she could spend the right number of years afterward ashamed and still curious? Everyone had these stories, it seemed. The rude older boy who stuck his hand in your jeans. The beer-enhanced groping in junior high that might mean "third base." She'd even have settled, for God's sake, for the solitary horse-back ride through the dusty canyon one afternoon, when the animal's seductive rhythms brought on a hot-faced excitement.

Nothing. None of it. Flannery had been kissed and embraced, she'd been dated and danced with, as any pretty teen might be. There had been park fumbles and party fondles, the unexpected encounter with slobber, and within that encounter a thin, faint hint of excitement. But she'd certainly never known *orgasm*. She had to read about it first, typically, and had then, curious girl, set out to look for it.

At college, thousands of miles from home and the familiar, under safe cover of darkness, she finally found it. Over and over. Oh! So *that's* what they meant. Once Flannery found it, she couldn't stop wanting that pleasure, enjoying the sound of her own short breaths in the quiet night air. More. Over. Again. She had to make up for lost years.

Yet, even as she grew ever more learned in this new field of knowledge, she knew that something was missing. She needed someone else—a face, a figure—to take with her into the fantasy.

Why was Cheryl always around? Why could Flannery not shake her for the shy Puerto Rican girl on the floor below, who spoke with the low lilt of a poet; or even for bleached, surferish Nick with an earring, whose laughter she often seemed to sit next to while eating, though they'd yet to trade anything besides names and home states and complaints about the mold-ridden dorm rooms?

"Hi, Cheryl." Flannery was too tired to fight it this morning. She'd had a long night: she'd gone to a late screening of a crime caper that starred a feisty black-haired actress—whose leather-clad antics had kept Flannery up, after, back alone in her room. Her stiff fingers plucked now at the cranberries embedded in the top of a sugar-crusted muffin. She needed their vitamin C.

"What are you doing here?" Cheryl stood over her at the table. "Aren't you coming?"

"To what?" Sometimes college seemed merely an endless exhausting string of appointments. She needed a nap already, and it was not yet ten o'clock.

"*Section*." Cheryl pulled Flannery's sweater. The girl couldn't stop touching her. It was beginning to get out of hand. "For *Criticism*. Remember?"

"Oh God. Yeah. Thanks for reminding me." Flannery swallowed a few more chunks of cranberry muffin, took a gulp of weak coffee, and cleared her dishes. "Thanks. I'd completely forgotten."

They ambled over to a remote classroom across some foreign lawn. Flannery had to follow Cheryl's lead there. She ought to be grateful to her annoying hallmate, really, for her organization, and to prove that she was, Flannery allowed Cheryl to flutter on chirpily about a date she'd had the night before with a cute Iowan named Doug.

Tuesday Anne. Right. And here it was, Tuesday. *If this is Tuesday, it must be Anne*, Flannery thought, entertaining herself sleepily with bad jokes of this kind.

Doug was still in the air between them as the two women found the classroom, but for Flannery their entrance was accompanied by a loud internal sound effect.

Fuck.

She had to be Anne, of course: Anne had to be *her*. Smaller in the large beige classroom, but just as vivid, as mouth-perfect; just as burn-bright. Sitting at the head of a broad seminar table looking through a folder of papers, handing a sheaf to a student on her right to pass around, giving Flannery a moment to look at her.

She had the same serenely clear skin, the same slick red-dark hair, straight to her chin. And she wore the same outfit. Black leather jacket, in a cut trim and feminine rather than motorcycle-like, silver-zippered in a few strategic places; close-fitting blue jeans, studiously faded; pointed, pretty, argumentative boots. Not high-heeled or spiky, and not black either—a deep animal brown—but certainly the kind that were made for walking. They brought a Nancy Sinatra shiver to Flannery's hunched shoulders.

She stopped in the doorway, before she'd been seen. "I can't . . . I forgot . . ." she stuttered to Cheryl.

"What? Come on. This is the right room. I recognize the lady."

That's no lady, Flannery wanted to say, but she kept quiet as Cheryl dragged her over to a corner chair. At least the closer seats were filled, so they could sit farther away, near the window. If worse came to worst, Flannery could always jump out of it. The act might have a certain poetry. Might reveal, all too late, her sensitivity to Criticism.

It had to happen. Once seated, Flannery tried to busy herself with her educational equipment, but all she really needed was a notebook and a pen. She placed these in front of her. Someone handed her another printed sheet of paper, which listed due dates for papers, Anne's office hours, the exam schedule. It had to happen. There was nowhere else to turn. Flannery finally looked up.

And there she was, her tormentor, watching Flannery cannily with her glorious green eyes.

"All right, kids," the instructor began, getting the irony in at the very beginning. "Welcome to the wide world of criticism. There are a lot of you, which is delightful, but it means extra work for me. Your job is to be able to distinguish, by the end of the semester, Derrida from de Man, Henry Louis Gates from Harold Bloom; mine is to be able to distinguish one of you from another. Sadly, that means roll call. Pretend you're in the army. Amy Adamson? David Bernstein? . . ." And on she went, stopping after each name for a moment with each face, to lock it in her memory.

Inevitably she reached "Flannery Jansen," a name that caused her to look around the room with a disbelieving half-smile. Flannery had no choice but to raise her pen in reluctant self-identification.

"You're *Flannery*?" she repeated, bringing the rose of embarrassment once more to Flannery's pale face. "Well, that gives you a kind of head start, doesn't it, in the literature department?"

She carried on, mercifully, so that Flannery could keep her head down and devote the rest of the hour to not listening to anything else the woman had to say. The instructor went over the material of the first week's lecture, adorning and explaining and encouraging questions. In spite of Flannery's stubborn ears she couldn't help noticing that the words were uttered with an easy wit and grace. She also couldn't help noticing—it was her fingers that noticed it—a taunting intimacy between their two names. Without thinking about it, while not listening, Flannery decorated the instructor's name on the printout with some extra letters, so that ANNE became FL-ANNE-RY. Having seen with horror what she'd done, she then had to scribble over the entire name, rather violently. Finally, ANNE ARDEN was wiped out altogether, lost to a block of blue ink.

Class was ending. Thank God. People were standing. The ordeal was almost over. Flannery leaned over to Cheryl.

"I'm going to have to switch into a different section."

"You are? Why?"

"I just—can't do this one. I remembered I have something else that conflicts." She was not about to explain her reasons to distracted, Doug-stunned Cheryl.

"Oh well," said Cheryl, and left in a down-jacketed huff, puffed up in offense. "What*ever.*"

Flannery planned to make it up to her later; perhaps by sharing some sweet dried apricots Flannery's mother had sent her from home.

"Excuse me."

Flannery stood a good two feet away from where the beautiful woman still sat. Her voice had to be a little louder to cover the table's distance between them; she would not risk anything like proximity.

"I have a problem."

The instructor looked up with the mocking expression Flannery knew well enough from the other day's uneaten breakfast. The TA—Anne—was silent, but her eyes weren't. *I know you have a problem*, they said clearly. *I can see it.*

"I can't do Tuesdays. I didn't realize when I signed up for this section. How do I switch?"

The woman nodded, with mirth-suppressed seriousness. "Many more people are taking this class than we expected." She sounded friendly, collegial. "We'll probably have to add some sections. I'm sure I'll run another one. How are Thursday afternoons for you?"

"Bad," Flannery said, so fast it was clear she couldn't have thought about it. "I could do Mondays, though. With the other guy—Bob." She realized that the change might mean sacrificing Animal Behavior. So much for her science credit.

"Hmmm. Monday may be filled up by now." But the instructor was getting bored with this teasing game. She put her papers away in the folder and said in a more businesslike tone, "Talk to us at the end of the next lecture. Everyone will be reshuffling their schedules, but Bob and I will stay after and try to figure out how to accommodate you all. We want to keep our little darlings happy."

"Well." Her rudeness freed Flannery somehow. "We're all slavishly grateful to you, obviously."

She turned to go, but not before seeing that elegant head snap back up. As Flannery moved toward the door she heard that voice again. It seemed huskier now, with a nicotined rasp. Oh, of course. It wasn't enough that Tuesday Anne was beautiful; she had to have a sexy voice, too, one that Flannery might think about dying for.

"Where did you get a name like Flannery, anyway?" the voice asked Flannery's walking-away back.

Flannery shrugged, her signature gesture, on her way out the door. She only half-turned her head.

"From my mom."

The voice followed Flannery across the high-walled courtyarded campus, in and out of the stacks of the vast library, down the corridors of the fake-Gothic buildings. It became familiar with her educational geographies, just as Flannery herself did. She heard this voice in the granite-enclosed shower within the white-tiled bathroom (where driven girls performed their furtive rituals of purging); in the stained-glass-windowed dining hall, where she finally met surferish Nick. Loudest of all, she heard it on the thickening, fall-scattered streets, where she walked for solace and thought, quiet spells when she made sure she was keeping up with her learnings and changes. As October took shape, Flannery looked back on her September self as if on a previous generation, one born long before the modern world had begun, when there was still innocence. (Flannery felt she had lost hers on her first trip to the Doodle.) If the then-early yellows and greens had stunned her, the trees' colors grew only more glorious—mango and marigold, pumpkin and cantaloupe; even, in places, the pomegranate she'd hoped for—till Flannery wondered, numbly, whether they might stop her heart altogether, or blind her cold-tearing eyes.

She continued to hear Anne's voice in her ear. How was this possible? Flannery hadn't spoken to Anne since transferring out of her section into Bob's. Bob made Criticism painless, if not entirely compelling. He had the greedy eyes of a squirrel and was brown-snaggle-haired, with a rough cut of near-beard almost like side-burns. It gave him the appearance of a German leftist from the 1970s, which in turn gave him a nice European authority as he deconstructed for the bewildered students the games and feints of Derrida and the others. Bob enjoyed guy-talk and wordplay and performing faux-casual postmodern tricks, like giving semiotic readings of the food sold at McDonald's ("What signifies *McNugget*?"), or making fanciful claims as to the hidden subver-sions of Hollywood blockbusters. He claimed that those beefy-muscled action heroes could teach Hélène Cixous a thing or two about the meaning of the masculine.

Flannery didn't actually hear Anne, but once a week she saw her sitting at the front of the lecture hall. She witnessed Anne handing out the exam questions for the midterm. While Bradley held forth, Flannery watched Anne brush her hand through her hair and sensed her fingers twitching for nicotine; she noted her occasional taking of notes; and she took in the curve of her leather jacket as she leaned over sometimes to whisper jokes to Bob, who nodded and grinned. Flannery couldn't hear the voice or the jokes, mostly couldn't even see Anne's face, just the copper cut of her hair. But by a trick of her mind she could feel the woman's breath in her ear, which made her own note-taking impossible, and melted her deeper, uselessly, into her seat.

Cheryl dropped Criticism, thank God, so Flannery was freed of any connection to Tuesday Anne. There was another class member, a sharp Korean woman named Susan, who was good to talk to in disentangling theory but had an unfortunate habit of telling bewitching tales of her TA—who happened to be Anne. "She's so smart and funny, I swear to God she's better than Bradley," Susan had said once to Flannery. Reluctantly, Flannery excused herself out of their study sessions together as a way of trying to regain her balance.

She couldn't do it. It was unregainable. Flannery looked for Anne on campus even when she swore to herself that she wasn't, and she found Anne in places she never would have looked. She saw Anne's face through the window of a Japanese restaurant, where she was eating sushi with an unseeable companion; she saw Anne waiting to cross the street, sipping from a Styrofoam cup, looking impatient; and she saw Anne once in the all-night convenience store, buying cigarettes, when Flannery was there for detergent. Dressed in her laundry outfit—baggy gray sweats and her sheepskin boots, for God's sake, with a dumb-logoed sweatshirt—Flannery had had to flee empty-handed, and was forced afterward to beg some Cheer from a friend.

Then there were the patterns Flannery had inadvertently noticed. Anne seemed to breakfast regularly at the Yankee Doodle, so that any morning Flannery "accidentally" passed the tiny diner, an internal battle waged whether or not she should look inside. (She had once been burned by Anne's looking up, too, so their eyes met; humiliated, Flannery had to skip that day's lecture.) Anne held office hours on Fridays and could be seen crossing the wide lawn toward the rust-colored corner building in the mid-afternoon light. And there was a section of the library—the underground, red-lit bunkerlike section, near the coffee and candy machines—where Anne could be found nights, reading and smoking. Occasionally with someone, often alone. Every time Flannery went to the library she had to ask herself: Are you really going to study? Or are you planning to find an excuse to go buy a Twix bar? Worse—are you going to try to study, only to torment yourself with cravings for chocolate, which you can't then satisfy as it might mean seeing her face?

The simplest solution to this extravagant problem would have been for Flannery herself to drop Criticism. The approach of the drop deadline made her pretend to consider it. But, she argued with herself, she liked Criticism. Really! It was interesting. She was learning a lot; and she had done so well on the midterm. It seemed stupid to stop taking it just because of a slightly distracting infatuation, which would doubtless pass soon enough. Besides, it was a body of knowledge, she felt sure, she'd one day be glad to have.

But what did she want, really? What did she imagine?

It wasn't as if, truth be told—and in the overheated darkness of her narrow room, she could tell the truth, at least to herself—Flannery knew. She did not know what she wanted. At a certain late point her mind willfully gave out, apologizing its way into a vague shrug of silence.

Do you want to have sex with that woman? Flannery tried to ask herself bluntly, staring at the dark ceiling, which vibrated with the loud explorations of her upstairs neighbor and his girl-friend. Flannery tried to shock herself into acknowledging a sexual awakening. Maybe that's what this was—she had heard of such things. Do you mean to tell me you're a lesbian? she demanded. Is that it?

She had seen the signs around campus. There were signs up for everyone: Latinos and African Americans, Avant-garde Musicians and Bridge Players. In the post office, collecting lifeline letters from her high-school friends, who scribbled to her intensely from their exiles elsewhere, Flannery had noticed a bright purple sheet of paper stuck to the tape-and-tack-scarred wall. "Gay and Lesbian Student Meeting. FRESHMEN WELCOME!" The notice seemed slightly sinister and predatory to the prude lurking within her. She did not think about going to the meeting, but she found herself curious—mildly—about what sorts of people would be there.

The word didn't appeal to her. "Lesbian." She didn't like the sound of it. It sounded slippery and gummy, or slightly nasal, like people with adenoid problems. Besides, if her back was against the wall, Flannery would have to admit that she found José, who was in her Intro to Art History class, also cute, handsome—whatever.

It was just— This much Flannery could say to herself, aloud, could allow into the full light of her wakeful hours.

It's just simple. It's simple.

I just want to kiss her.

Dreams said otherwise.

Inevitably.

That is what dreams love to do. Taunt you with a bawdy vividness you have forbidden by day. Rummage through your mind's closets, dig through its storage drawers, finding hopes or perceptions you had not known you harbored. Colors you had not consciously seen. Jokes of a cleverness you had never suspected yourself capable of.

As the nights grew colder and November crept stealthily on, Flannery's dreams grew hotter. Less inhibited. They threw off their coverings, stripping down at night even as Flannery was layering more on by day. As Flannery began to sense what might eventually be meant by *winter*, her dreams headed resolutely toward a bare-skinned summer.

Once, Anne was a small black terrier, and Flannery was stroking her. Cautiously.

Once, Flannery walked in on Anne and Nick. In her own room. Somehow she did not mind, but wished they had not chosen her room for their embraces.

Once, Flannery was still in Anne's class. Bob was furious. She handed her paper in late and got a bad grade.

Once—

But that one caused a prickling flush when Flannery thought of it, a clutch in her gut and an undeniable heat in her thighs. She'd swallowed hard when she remembered it the next innocent morning. That one: she had to censor that one. In an effort to keep the internal peace.

They were—

It was—

And then, when she—

No, no. That one, without doubt, had to be censored.

Flannery couldn't see any immediate solution to any of it but to dance. So she danced.

Anywhere she could. She danced at cramped freshmen parties in dorm rooms, at which people paired off with a prompt urgency brought on by the beat and the general beer-cloud of conviction that that's what they were there for. She danced in daring, off-campus apartments on dark streets, where the students were older, the music was better, and Flannery saw two men kissing for the first time in her life. She even accompanied Nick—she and the bleach-headed math major had become wry outsider friends—to a nearby club, where up-and-coming bands tried out their new songs on effervescent students.

Flannery did not dance in order to pair off, which sometimes baffled her partners. For a while she would pay attention to who-ever was dancing across from her, whether man or woman; she would nod, thrust her shoulders, slink her hips forward in sync with the other one's movements. While dancing, she forgot her awkward feet and virginal modesty. She came closer to moving with the freedom she dreamed about. The rooms were hot, humid with gin breath and sweat and pickup lines shouted into ears, which were answered with grinning nods, as if the listener had heard, when, crowd-deafened, they mostly hadn't. Like everyone else, Flannery wore scanty tops and jeans, sleeveless T-shirts and leggings: clothing that clung, and encouraged others' hungering intentions. She was wanted. She knew it, a little, in the back of her shy mind, but she kept her distance and somehow stayed out of arm's reach.

There always came a time in the night or the dance when Flannery retreated, fell back into herself. She'd close her eyes and go. Her partners, her company could feel it, as if they had just lost this lean, sultry girl over some unseen edge, and all that was left before them was a pretty shell, a body-ghost, someone empty to their touch. Sometimes it was so noticeable that they did touch her—her arm or her shoulder—to bring her back. She'd smile, open her eyes, and maybe toss her head, snap her fingers, take a few steps forward or back. But it was clear she remained unreached. And mysteriously unreachable.

There was someone with her when she danced, though. When Flannery closed her eyes, lost her head to the drink and the music, there was one person she had in her mind, one person for whom she dipped and writhed, swayed and swung. When her hands shaped the air, it was that person's form they were seeking.

Then, one night, as one of her favorite songs throbbed to its close, Flannery suddenly opened her eyes, wide. Two in the morning, drunk and steamy, in a stranger's friendly, frenzied apartment.

And there she was.

In front of her. As if Flannery had imagined her into life. As if her creative powers were, after all, that strong.

"Hi, Flannery."

Anne's face, in the low party light, seemed shockingly benign. Then again, Flannery was drunk.

"Hi."

So she didn't wear the leather jacket every single waking minute: here she was bare-shouldered, in a sleeveless white cotton vest. Black jeans. Simple. But her shoulders seemed so vulnerable, exposed, that Flannery had an odd gallant impulse. Surely they should be covered, those delicate shoulders, with a wrap or a coat. Even a protective arm. Anne seemed so small here.

"Great party," Flannery said, stupidly. But what else could she say?

"Yeah. Do you know Cameron?" Anne gestured toward a blond, floppy-haired figure who was leaning lustfully into a short black man beside him.

Flannery nodded, smiled, and shrugged in some vague combination that she hoped didn't commit her one way or another. Actually, she had no idea whose party this was; she couldn't even remember who had brought her here. Where had she put her drink? Down on some speaker somewhere?

"You looked like you were getting into the music," Anne said. Still smiling! What was the matter with her? "I didn't mean to interrupt." She glanced at the friend Flannery had been dancing with, who was now moving slinkily over to someone else.

"No, no. I was—just getting ready to go, anyway. It's late." Flannery wiped the sweat from her face. She felt so tall, standing over Anne. It seemed all wrong.

"You don't have to leave just because I'm here." The woman gazed at her with something more like the expected sarcasm. "I'm not grading you, you know."

"Yeah." Flannery couldn't figure out where to put her hands: she had nothing to hold on to. "Listen—do you want a drink? I'm going to get one. I'm dying of thirst."

Blurred moments later, Flannery was standing over a rickety kitchen table that had been flash-flooded with alcohol: an unruly mixture of rum, gin, and vodka and a variety of drifting, bubbly mixers. Dead half-limes and -lemons had washed up on the shore; some red plastic cups swam tipsily sideways in the current. Others were scattered upright on other surfaces, but they were all half-filled, or lipstick-stained, or choked with damp cigarette butts. None were clean. The scene was vomitous, generally, and Flannery could feel the dangerous rise in her throat of whatever her own poison had been—vodka and grapefruit juice, probably, which someone somewhere had told her was called a Salty Dog.

She could leave now, before it came to staggering around looking for the bathroom. No. *No.* Flannery breathed. She moved over to the window. She wasn't as bad as all that. If she could just pause here a minute; then she could come to terms, slowly, with her inability to find that wretchedly beautiful woman a drink. Or she could just sneak away altogether, to escape her shame.

"I thought you might have gotten lost."

Here she was again! Jesus Christ. She had followed Flannery in here.

"Or that you were planning to ditch me." Anne's voice was sly.

"Oh no. Never! You know I'd never do that." Flannery kept her cheek close to the pane to stay cool. What had she just said? "No. I was just stopping for a minute to get some air."

"Good idea. It's so damned stuffy here. Let's open the other one, too."

But the other window seemed stuck. The two women had to stand together and push to overcome its reluctance. Flannery could see the taut line of Anne's forearm muscle as they tried to maneuver it.

It gave, suddenly, so that Anne fell forward, fast, into the icy onrush of night. Flannery instinctively grabbed her shoulders to hold her back—the apartment was on the fourth floor—though there was no real danger of her falling through.

They both drew away from the window then, back into the warmer party air. Each of them shivered with relief, and with cold. Anne looked at her with a smile of an unnamable kind on her moist lips.

"Well, thank you, Flannery," she said, in mock solemnness. She held her hand out for her hero to shake on. "You saved my life."

And then what?

Flannery's memory ended exactly there, and no amount of gray dining-hall coffee the next morning could bring any more back. "You saved my life," Anne had said, ironically of course; maybe she'd even added "My hero!" to underline the joke. And then—what? Kissed her? Inconceivable. That, Flannery would have remembered. Lit a cigarette, shook her hand, said good night, sent Flannery on her way? Dully plausible. Or had she, rather, laughed savagely, hyenalike, knowing of Flannery's impossible crush, which that hot-handed clasp of the shoulders made clumsily obvious?

But maybe this crush wasn't impossible. Maybe—God knows, it was hard to credit it—maybe it was possible, after all.

Hadn't she complimented Flannery on her dancing? Or had she? Maybe Flannery had made that up. Or, more likely, overinterpreted. Anne said something like *Oh, go ahead, keep dancing*, which Flannery had feverishly redrafted as *My God, you enticing creature, you must dance for me and only for me.*

"Hey, Jansen."

It was a disheveled Nick, bearing a bowl of cereal. He had taken to calling her by her last name. Flannery couldn't remember why anymore. This seemed to be what college was about—learning a vast amount, thus triggering an onset of chronic memory loss.

"Hey."

"You look kind of wrecked. If you don't mind my saying so."

"Yeah." Flannery drank some more dreg-heavy coffee. As if that would help. "Listen. Were you at that party last night? In that guy Cameron's apartment?"

"Was I there!" He laughed, before shoveling cereal into his mouth. He paused to chew milkily, and Flannery had to look away. Her nausea was returning. "You *are* wrecked. I'm the one who took you there. Remember?"

"Oh yeah. Right." She did, too. Sort of. She could imagine it, anyway. "So. Here's my question. I didn't do anything stupid, did I, before I left? That you saw?"

"Jansen, Jansen, Jansen." He shook his head sadly. Over a mouthful of Sugar Pops he seemed to consider tormenting her with a series of amusing lies about her embarrassing escapades, but decided benevolently against it. "No. Relax. All I saw was you dancing with some red-headed chick in a tank top, till God knows what hour."

"Dancing? With her?"

"Yep." He thought about it for a minute. And swallowed. "Yep. She was hot."

It seemed criminal to finally have the raw stuff of fantasy—dancing, with Anne, for pity's sake!—and not be able to remember it. Flannery could not forgive herself. She felt sure that under hypnosis she would be able to retrieve the images. Were they close? What songs did they dance to? How did Anne move?

Then again, Nick might have made that up.

Or maybe just embellished, unaware of how critical accuracy was here. After all, he was probably drunk, too. Maybe she and Anne had one single dance together. That was probably it, and Flannery could just about re-create a montage of smiles and bare arms (she remembered with heartbreaking clarity the curve of Anne's shoulders), some general moving around to something like music. Flannery remained completely blank, however, on what idiocies she might have uttered, what confessions freely given, what sloppy compliments slurred into that exquisite ear.

It was impossible to go to class, obviously. How could Flannery be in the same room with her, not knowing what had gone on? When the Thursday of the lecture dawned, Flannery was all set to skip it. Then she ran into Susan Kim, who reminded her that it was the last class before the Thanksgiving break, when Bradley would be talking about the extra reading they were supposed to do in preparation for their long-paper assignment. Flannery had to go. Why hadn't she dropped the damn class? Who needed Criticism, anyway? She went so far as to place a desperate call to someone in Admin to find out if it was truly, absolutely, too late to drop the class now. She got an earful of accented attitude from a secretary ("That's why we have *deadlines*," as if she were stupid), which was enough—almost—to make Flannery break the phone, pack her bags, and head back West. Life was so peaceful there, by comparison.

She went to class late. That was her compromise. In through a rear door, five minutes late, so that Anne would be safely sitting up front, her back to Flannery. For eighty tense minutes Flannery took jittery erratic notes, which she later found mostly unintelligible. Five minutes before the class ended, she packed away her notebook and got ready to go. Susan looked at her quizzically. The professor was just then reaching the heart of what he was hoping from them in their long papers (none of which he would ever read; that was the privilege of the teaching assistants). He listed important pitfalls for them to avoid, tips on how to find something original to say. Flannery missed all of it. To Susan she shrugged with a half-smile and mouthed, *Doctor's appointment*. Susan nodded and went back to her own notes.

Flannery left. So relieved not to have to see Anne that on her way out she slammed the door inadvertently. She could hear its loud, wooden reverberations echo through the Critical classroom as she made her lucky escape to the world outside.

There was no question on Friday whether Flannery wanted any proximity to the rust-colored corner building where—she couldn't make herself forget this—Anne held her afternoon office hours (3–5 p.m., Room 303). She didn't. She didn't want to be anywhere near there. She stopped at the post office, which was ghost-townishly deserted already, most students having left for their Thanksgiving vacation. Flannery had a pretty good haul: a Thanksgiving gift pack from her mother, two letters, and a heavy envelope sent via campus mail. Nick had recently discovered the cost-free joys of campus mail and had taken to sending Flannery ridiculous items, "just to keep them busy"—the freshmen face book, his winter hat, a packet of Alka-Seltzer Plus ("for effective relief of headache with upset stomach which may be due to excessive food or drink"—gone over in helpful yellow highlighter).

Flannery bundled up her items and took them away to the bookstore/café where she intended to enjoy them slowly, with a cup of decent coffee, while not thinking about anybody's office hours, or dance movements, or black leather jacket, or lack of black leather jacket. While not listening to the music playing in the background, which sounded uneasily familiar—a dance tune she thought might have been playing that night in Cameron's apartment. Flannery worked to drive the music out of her head.

Her friends' letters were entertaining, filled with familiar accounts of parties, studies, sudden romances. The package from her mother was cute. A pretty scarf, some candy corn, of all things (oh: left over from her Halloween stash, it must have been), and a card that said brightly, "Can't wait to see you at Christmas! Enjoy your Turkey Day, Honey." Flannery had been invited, dutifully, to enjoy Thanksgiving dinner in New York by her invisible roommate, a pre-med who wore pink sweaters and with whom Flannery rarely spoke. Nick, too, had mentioned that his family would be on the Cape, and she'd be welcome to join them. ("They're neurotic as hell, but the food's good." It was a time of charity toward others.) She had not yet decided what she was going to do.

What had he sent her this time? Flannery opened the campus mail envelope. A book. Something kitsch, no doubt. Flannery turned it over, surprised. Poems! That seemed serious for Nick. By someone named Marilyn Hacker. *Love, Death, and the Changing of the Seasons.*

Inside, a note:

I brought this to give you in class today, but I didn't see you. Beware delinquency!
Something you said the other night made me think you'd enjoy these. A little extra reading for you over the break. Don't worry—they won't be on the final.

Yours,
Anne

Before Flannery had a chance to take in the import of this note, someone sat down at her table. Loud, in a diminutive kind of way, and trailing cigarette smoke. Flannery's cheeks were, she felt quite certain, cranberry red as she looked up.

Into the bright, almond-eyed face of Susan Kim.

She was laughing. "Oh my God!" she said, smoking, unjacketing, and rolling up her sleeves more or less all at once. "I am so in love with my TA, it's not even funny."

Too many stimuli all at once. But Flannery did do one thing immediately, instinctively—she hid the book from Susan. Her eagerness to open and read it was so ferocious she had to sit on her hands.

"Who?" she asked, with a casualness that she felt deserved a medal. "You mean—that woman—Anne?"

Susan inhaled deeply, nodded, and exhaled politely to the side. "I get so hot and bothered around her. You know. That jacket! Those boots! I was just in there with her talking about the term paper."

That jacket, Flannery thought; yes. Those boots: I know them.

"She said we should meet for a drink sometime."

"She did?" *And did she dance with you? Did she give you some poems?*

"Yeah, but I don't know. With your TA? Wouldn't that be kind of weird? God, do you think she's gay?"

Flannery felt a thick choke of jealousy around her throat. She shrugged, then coughed, violently. "Maybe. You know, I—I wouldn't know."

"Hey, are you okay? You look a little—" Susan saw the mail scattered like torn leaves before Flannery on the table, and concern crossed her kind face. "Did you just get some bad news or something?"

"No." Flannery cleared her throat, coughed again, took a sip of coffee. "Just come candy corn from my mother," she croaked. "Do you want some?"

"Sure. Thanks." Susan put a cupped palm out for some fluorescent orange-and-yellow cones, popped a few into her mouth, then said somberly, "How was your doctor's appointment?"

"My what? Oh, okay. It turned out to be nothing. Listen"— Flannery saw the clock over the fiction section. It was just after five—"you know what? I'm sorry. I just realized, I've got to get going. I'm late for something."

Susan was a little hurt, Flannery could tell. She must think Flannery disliked her. Flannery tried to make up for her rudeness with a friendly, compensating gesture.

"Here, have some more candy corn. It's good for you." She poured a generous portion out onto the table. "The Indians brought candy corn to the Pilgrims, you know. As a peace offering." Susan did not look convinced. "And to help them get through the bitterly cold winters."

It turned out to be pretty difficult, simultaneously reading a volume of poetry and jogging two blocks and half a courtyard to the rust-colored building. The poems became word-blurs as her eyes watered with the cold, speedy air.

Once inside, Flannery ran up two flights of broad marble stairs to the third floor, where she assumed Room 303 would be. (She'd had the number emblazoned on her memory since that first class handout.) But nothing at this university was ever so simple. The place was a maze. The third floor was occupied entirely by classrooms. She ran up another flight, dashed down a corridor, stalled out in a blind alley, retraced her steps, was about to bark with frustration, then half-skidded round a corner and there—thank God!—was Room 303.

Without thinking about it she knocked loudly, her hand emphatic with urgency. What if Anne had gone?

"Jesus Christ!" She saw now that though the door was closed, the light was on. The voice was startled and abrupt. "I hear you. Can you please wait outside till we've finished?"

Flannery was silent. She realized—for some reason the possibility hadn't occurred to her as she jogged—that someone else was still in there with her.

"Who *is* it?" Now irritated, exhausted. "My office hours ended ten minutes ago." A pause, followed by laughter. Then, said more softly—intimately, it seemed to Flannery—"Maybe I scared them away. Oh well!"

Flannery leaned against the wall, catching her breath. She heard a mumble of voices carry on their interrupted conversation.

Quietly, quietly, Flannery pulled the book of poems out of the envelope again and thumbed through it. Furtively: as if it were a bomb-construction manual or an advance, sneak copy of the final. A line from an early poem caught her attention.

I bet you blush all over when you come.

Flannery closed her eyes and the book. Her legs were weak: it was a good thing the wall she was leaning against wasn't.

Maybe this was a bad idea. She could walk away; tiptoe back down the stairs and out of the maze. It would be as if she had never been there at all.

The door opened and light spilled out, catching the sleeve of her jacket.

"Oh God. Is someone still waiting there? You'd better send them in. Come *in!*"

Brittle with impatience.

At least—small mercies—Flannery did not know the shuffling male student who had had his turn before hers and who nodded to her, sympathetically, on his way out.

She went in, closed the door.

"Flannery!"

"Hi."

She sat down, mostly because she had to, or her knees might give way. Anne's face was flushed with surprise. That, at least, was gratifying.

"I thought maybe you had already flown the nest. Or, you know what I mean, flown back to the nest." Was it possible that Anne was nervous? "The way you fledglings do, around Thanksgiving."

"I'm staying here."

"Not for the whole week?"

"No. My roommate invited me to go to New York. Another friend asked me to go to the Cape. I haven't decided which I'll do."

"That's where I'm going. New York." Well then: that decided it. "I can't wait to get the hell out of here." But Anne seemed to feel she'd said too much. "So. I take it you're not here to talk about your term paper? I'm not Bob, as you've probably noticed."

"I know."

There was a pause. Anne waited, still as a cat. Her eyes had again that translucent intensity that Flannery found infinitely distracting. The pause expanded with Flannery's silence, till Anne finally said, "Look, I have to—" and Flannery spoke at the same time, right over her.

"Do you want to go out for a drink?"

That shocked her.

"A drink? When—now?"

When? Flannery hadn't thought that far ahead. "Sure—now. Or—later."

Flannery watched the possibility travel across the instructor's face, like a breeze. What it would take: letting go of responsibility; release; the chance of risk.

"Sure, Flannery. I'll have a drink with you," she said. "What the hell? Let's go."

They were both startled into silence by their daring decision, and conversation between them stuttered like a broken faucet. Flannery followed Anne out of the building and into the gray dampening streets. She had no idea where they were going, and in spite of Anne's shorter legs had to jog some to keep up.

"So—" Flannery kept her head down as they passed the brightly lit bookstore/café, where Susan Kim might lurk. "You had a lot of students come by about their papers?"

An immediate cringe. Why talk about that?

"Yes."

"It must get a little repetitive after a while, all these paper ideas."

"Mmmhmm."

A spell of brisk heel-chatter—Anne's. Flannery's, flat, were quiet.

"I guess it's a pretty key part of the class, though. The term paper."

Anne declined to dignify this vapidness with an answer. She was not going to make it any easier by speaking, apparently; leaving Flannery plenty of room to dig her own ample, comfortable grave.

"At least you don't have— I mean, at least you're free over this break."

"Not exactly. I have a paper of my own to write. I'm going to be on a panel at MLA at the end of December."

"MLA?"

"The Modern Language Association. Their year-end conference, where everyone in all kinds of fields, including me, prostrates themselves trying to get a job."

Of course! She had a life outside of Intro to Criticism. Flannery would have to remember that. She would have to bear that in mind.

"Well then, I'm glad I caught you before—"

"Here we go."

They were at the bar, thank God: the Anchor. Together they ducked out of the cold and into its dim jukeboxed interior. The warmth here, Flannery hoped, might stem the flow of her wintry inanities, and she'd find a way to make herself shut the hell up.

The bar was almost completely empty at that hour.

"At least we won't have a problem finding a table," Anne said.

"Yeah. It's probably good that no one's here." Flannery allowed the reminder to hover: this is a student-teacher meeting. We're not supposed to be doing this. It had the desired effect of throwing Anne a little off her rhythm. Anything, Flannery felt, to disrupt for a moment that stern assurance.

A plump, mannequin-faced barmaid came by, scrutinized Flannery, understood that she was underage; then asked anyway, with a skeptical drawl, "What are you having?"

Flannery ordered a White Russian. Anne started to comment, but checked herself and ordered a gin-and-tonic. When the barmaid had gone, she leaned over the table. Her eyes were fireflies, suddenly, of brightness.

"A White Russian?" she teased. "That's a kid's drink!"

Flannery shrugged, unembarrassed. She felt better in here. It was nice and dark, and the jukebox soothed with a series of Glenn Miller classics. "They taste good."

"I suppose it's a step up from a daiquiri."

"So what do grown-ups drink? Gin-and-tonics?"

"Yes, that. And other things. You'll have to learn."

"You'll have to teach me," Flannery dared. Before even having a sip! The barmaid brought their drinks, and they waited till she had retreated to continue.

"How old are you, Flannery?"

Anne's low voice caught at Flannery's throat. That voice: she wanted to own it. She looked away. "Seventeen."

"Seventeen!" The startlement was real. "My God. You shouldn't be drinking that! You should be drinking a Coke. You should be drinking a glass of *milk*. Your bones are still growing."

"So how old are you?" Flannery challenged.

"Ancient. Twenty-eight."

Twenty-eight. Like everything else, of course, it was perfect. It sounded wise; well traveled; sophisticated. Promise-filled.

"Well, cheers." Flannery lifted her glass, her own gray eyes alight now, she knew, with some unsuppressed delight in the company.

"Cheers," Anne answered. "To what?"

"To twenty-eight." Flannery clinked her glass to Anne's. "It's a beautiful age. In my opinion."

The word reached Anne and softened her. Warmth moved her mouth into a heart-shaped pleasure.

"Cheers," she replied again, with a sudden shyness that made Flannery swoon.

"To seventeen." Clink. "Ditto."

They drank, as Glenn Miller played on.

"Thanks for the Marilyn Hacker book. I haven't had a chance to look at it yet."

Something like relief loosened Anne's shoulders. "She's a wonderful poet. Deceptive—a great formalist, under the conversational style." Anne sipped her drink. "Something you said the other night about your love of rhythm made me think you'd enjoy her."

Flannery thanked God in heaven that she'd never have to know what she might have said about her love of rhythm.

"What other poetry do you like?" she deflected. So they talked poetry for a while; or Anne did. Flannery had to plead ignorance. As in so many things. Poetry hadn't, she explained, made it onto her first, introductory platter. Anne asked her what had, besides Criticism. "Revolution, Art History, World Fiction. I was taking Animal Behavior, but had to drop it."

"That's an eclectic mix."

"Well, I'm undeclared. —In my major, I mean."

They both let that pass.

"So: World Fiction. Who do you read in that? What is 'World Fiction,' anyway?"

"Fiction—from the world, I guess."

"As opposed to fiction from other worlds?"

"Yeah." Flannery liked the joke. "That's probably the kind I'll write."

"Ah." Anne took another sip of her drink, rummaged around in her pockets for her cigarettes. "You're hoping to write?"

"Not hoping to, exactly." Flannery looked puzzled. "I just do."

"And isn't it a little—daunting, if you write, to be saddled with a name like Flannery?"

Flannery's shoulders rose involuntarily, their customary punctuation. "I'm used to it. I mean, I'm used to my name. At least I'm not called, you know, Jamaica."

"That's true," Anne said with a tilt of her head. "But then, who is?"

"Oh—Jamaica Kincaid. We're reading her for World Literature. She's incredible. I love her."

Interest sharpened Anne's focus. She thought, maybe, of bluffing recognition, then decided against it. "I don't know her work."

"You don't?" Flannery said, a little too eagerly. "You'd love it. God, it's so crazy, and lyrical. Beautiful."

Then she quieted down and looked into her milky drink, embarrassed. Having, as usual, given too much away.

So that she had the bad luck to miss the gold that had come into Anne's eyes, which suggested otherwise.

"So. Flannery."

Anne reached for her hard pack of cigarettes. From the box she slowly drew a Marlboro. With the other hand, she found her lighter.

"Do you have a boyfriend?"

After a flick of her thumb, she lit the cigarette, capped the lighter, and took a drag, watching Flannery through narrowed eyes.

Flannery sipped her drink.

She watched Anne smoke. Anne knew damn well how good she looked when she smoked. She was enjoying it. So was Flannery, who was reluctant to interrupt her. Also, she liked inhabiting this moment of suspense. Finally, though, she answered.

"No," she said. Then, after another pause: "Not at the moment."

Anne nodded slowly, almost unnoticeably. But the cigarette had dwindled to mostly ash: she had smoked it down fast.

"So," Flannery continued. "Anne."

But she had the disadvantage of having no cigarette. All she could do was stir around the last swallows of her thinning drink, clattering the melting ice cubes. She'd have to start smoking. There would be no other way through this.

"Do you have a boyfriend?" A slight, risky emphasis on the "you."

Anne waited. She stubbed out her cigarette slowly, thoroughly, crushing the sparks as though the most important thing right now was to make sure she didn't set fire to the Anchor Bar by leaving any of the butt alight.

"No," she said.

She took a sip, then licked the gin from her lips.

"Not at the moment."

The two women looked at each other, each wearing a small similar smirk. Flannery lifted her near-emptied drink for a last taste of vodka and cool Kahlúaed milk. Anne, seeing her, lifted hers, too, and simultaneously they said, as their glasses met in a low-pitched kiss:

"Cheers."

The White Russians were beginning to add up. She'd had only two, but so early in the day and on an empty stomach, they were threatening to produce a certain restlessness. It wasn't revolution yet, but it might get there, and Flannery was pretty sure she wanted to avoid that.

"I'd better go," she said, looking at her watch.

"Seven-thirty? We must be getting close to your bedtime."

"They close the dining halls. I wouldn't be able to get any dinner."

"Can't have that."

"Well, my bones are still growing. As you say."

Flannery thought she'd gotten the hang of the banter, finally; but then realized, with a small seizure of regret, that Anne was genuinely disappointed.

"Though I could stay—I mean, I have some ramen noodles in my room . . ."

"No. I have to go, too. I have to get ready for New York." She tidied up her relaxed face, and something of the hardness came back to the set of her mouth. She called the barmaid over so she could pay the check and wouldn't allow Flannery anywhere near it. Flannery felt humiliated, like a child.

"But you shouldn't—I mean, I asked *you*—" She retreated rapidly back into nervousness.

"Leave it, Flannery. I've got it."

Silenced.

Then, one last glitter. A flicker. A jewel in the eyes.

"Next round's on you. All right?"

A line that led, with a speed Flannery couldn't later reconstruct, into an awkward barlit embrace goodbye, serenaded by Glenn Miller; a bland, mutual wish for a happy Thanksgiving; and a going of separate ways, back on the melancholy early-evening street. Anne off to her mysterious elsewhere home and Flannery to the dining hall, to catch what scraps of dinner she could.

Where she could wonder, slowly, what had just happened.

Once she got there, of course, Flannery was far too overwrought to be hungry. The place was deserted, with most of the students gone now, and Flannery took a forlorn plate of congealing lasagna into a dim corner where she could sit privately with her treasured reliving of their encounter. Soon, though, she was discovered.

Flannery had almost forgotten about Cheryl, who seemed to have become consumed by Iowan Doug. Cheryl was not a person Flannery was prepared to talk to right now. How could Cheryl be equal to the magnitudes of life? The great swoops of passion, the certainty of heartbreak?

"Hey, Flannery. Haven't see you in a while."

"Yeah, hi. How's it going?"

She sat opposite Flannery with an overspilling bowl of salad-bar salad: yellowish broccoli heads and withered mushrooms struggling to stay on board a Lo-Cal Ranch–drenched mess, across which rust-brown BacoBits scattered guilty nuggets of flavor. Flannery took a cheesy bite of lasagna, not because she wanted any, but to make her own silent point, if only Cheryl knew it, about the dull folly of dieting.

"How've you been?"

"Fine. How about you?"

They traded news and Thanksgiving plans. Cheryl was flying West first thing in the morning—her parents were missing her so much, she said, adding endearingly, "I can't wait to see my dog!" Flannery explained her dilemma: whether to accept the offer of her roommate in New York or that of Nick on the Cape.

"So what's going on with you and Nick, anyway?" Cheryl's cheek dimpled with innuendo.

"Nick? Nothing." Flannery glanced around to see if he was nearby.

"Oh, come on. I keep seeing you two together. What's up?"

"Nothing, really. Anyway, Nick is—" Flannery started, then stopped, confused. She realized she'd never articulated the fact that Nick was gay. But he was, surely. Wasn't he? "I don't think Nick has those kinds of feelings for me. You know, we're just friends."

"That's not what he told Doug."

"What?" Flannery was unprepared for this.

"He told Doug he has a huge crush on you. Come on, it's obvious. You can't pretend you haven't noticed. And he's so cute! You'd make a great couple."

Flannery pushed her chair back abruptly. There was no way to do this gracefully, but she tried to extricate herself from the conversation, the dining hall, the nauseating congealed lasagna, with some bungled excuse.

Cheryl carried on. She was a determined character.

"Doug and I are going to the movies tonight, if you want to join us. Nick might come along, too."

"Thanks. You know, I'd love to, but—I've got some reading I've really got to get done."

Cheryl shook her head.

"Reading?" she said. This time even Cheryl didn't believe her. "Flannery, it's Thanksgiving break."

When she understood that the poems by Marilyn Hacker were about what they had seemed to be about—a passionate, illicit affair between two women, one older than the other—Flannery had to hide the book beneath her pillow. She got up and stretched her nervous arms. She walked to the window. She inhaled the sobering, icy air and exhaled a word, or sound, without meaning to. "God," it might have been, or "Fuck!," or possibly just a moan, a sigh from the anxious hollow of her unschooled heart.

She saw a figure, bleach-headed, crossing the half-lit courtyard. Flannery withdrew silently back into her room. It was Nick. She turned off the light, hoping he hadn't already checked for its reassurance, and then waited. Waited in the stillness—her roommate was off at the lab probably, as usual—for the knock on the door. He'd said something to her at breakfast about going out later for a drink or a movie, and she'd casually agreed. Yes, but that was a lifetime ago. Before she'd ever heard of Marilyn Hacker. Before she knew that Anne drank gin-and-tonics. Before she'd been issued a hasty promise: *The next round is on you.*

"Jansen?" He knocked on the door.

She pretended she was dead. Or elsewhere. ·

"Hey! Jansen!" He knocked again. "Are you in there? You're not passed out in a drunken stupor, are you?"

It was a joke, but she was insulted. What did he think of her?

"Shit." Then a pause, as he apparently scribbled a note on the message board her roommate had tidily stuck to their door the first week of the semester. (It was decorated with kittens, but there was nothing Flannery could do about that.) Flannery heard Nick's retreating steps but stayed still anyway. Wide-eyed. In the dark. What if he was waiting on the stairs? She couldn't meet him now. It was impossible.

Besides, she found the dark quite comforting. Quite relaxing. The dark had been a good friend to Flannery these past months. It had allowed her liberties she would never haven taken in the light, nor even when drunk. Alcohol did not open any genuinely new territories. It was merely a tongue-loosener, for a shy girl, and a dance-encourager, for someone who was just now, belatedly, starting to inhabit her body.

It was the dark that had taught her those tricks in the first place. Flannery took slow, deep breaths, feeling the familiar shape of her self.

It was the dark that, pulling at her now, allowed Flannery to recognize that she would have to meet those bold, terrifying poems with some voice of her own.

For hours in the dark, Flannery just thought. Felt. Heard words in her head and wondered which ones she'd choose to write down. A story or a poem? Or, best, neither? Over uncounted hours in the night her mind traveled the possibilities.

At an uncertain point in the underground journey, she heard her roommate come in. Midnight or one, probably. She heard the roommate go through her evening preparations, find her room, turn out the light. When the silence had stretched into a probable sleep, Flannery got up, turned on her own light again, and started to read more of the Hacker poems. They continued to make her jump and sweat. She put them back beneath her pillow, then turned off the light. Then breathed, thought, wondered further. Then turned on the light. Then wrote some lines on a piece of paper. Then rewrote them. Then went to the window and swallowed great gasps of night. Then came back to her desk. Then took the book from under the pillow, read a few more poems, returned them to her pillow. Then pulled out thick strands of her fair hair, dropping them without thinking onto the floor. Then read aloud what scratches she had so far, in a soft murmur, loud enough that only the writer in her could hear (and not the reined-in student or the timid stumbler). She nodded. Then raided her supply of Pop-Tarts. Then, as the black outside finally softened and gave way to indigo, she let her fingers tap out some lines, and printed them. When she saw and heard them in the rhythms she wanted, she cut them out, line by line. Then, her fingers trembling a little, she placed each thin strip carefully between different pages of a thin book. Her own copy of *At the Bottom of the River* by Jamaica Kincaid. When she was finished, the book was flagged with a dozen flickers of paper ends, like bookmarks.

By then it was light. Or something less like dark. Flannery's eyes itched with irritation at their tiredness, but her mind was wired. She knew what she had to do.

Miles to go before you sleep, she told herself. Then set out, with Pop-Tart-fed determination, on the long trek to the station.

PAGES FOR YOU

I'd like to pay your palms
the same favor that you pay these pages,
searching them for grooves and images
and the secret signs of hunger,
as you may scan these words
for hidden messages.
The lines of your hand might be a guide
to your gifts for pleasure,
or a clue to where you'll take me,
or a map of where I might take you.
They might show me the shape, already, of our fondest caress.

I'd like to pull your glorious boots off for you
so I could touch your toes, and heel, and
the vulnerable pale arch of your delicate foot.
I'd like to borrow from you those miles you've seen
and wear them in my own untraveled shoes.
I'd like to treat your feet with slow and ready fingers,
and bring you, unshod, to bliss,
while you recite for me some rhythms from these pages,
keeping us both in the motion of this unfolding story.

I plan to learn enough to read you like a book.
I plan to give this book to you and know you'll read it,
so our minds may meet across these pages,
in the colorful country of another writer's language,
where we can flourish in the knowledge
that we are learning how to speak to one another;
and so our mouths will know what to do
when they finally
come together.

It was not a comfortable place, but it invited sleep nonetheless. It was one of the long, curved benches that stretched the width of the high, vaulted old station, recently restored. Along these benches you felt both small and sleepy, connected as you were, inexorably, with all the other baffled and weary travelers passing through the quiet halls in the morning. It was still early. The light had been lemony and hesitant as Flannery walked over. It was not yet seven o'clock.

Flannery bought herself some sugared doughnuts and a cup of something trying to pass itself off as coffee and waited, sitting under the black arrivals-and-departures board. From time to time it fluttered busily like a flock of doves, wings flapping, letters and numbers passing, until the machinery settled on the information it wanted to impart. Trains to New York. Trains to Boston. A delayed train to Vermont. One, exotically, to Florida, via Washington, D.C.

It was the trains to New York Flannery had to keep her eye on. When she heard "Final boarding call!" for any of the New York trains, it was particularly important that she be alert. On the lookout for that familiar face, that cut of hair.

Three trains left for New York. Then a fourth. The place filled up with duffel-bagged students, hatted and scarved, readying themselves with joy or dread for their families. Flannery moved back several benches so she'd be less conspicuous; she knew some of these people (an Art Historian, a World Fictioner) and didn't especially want to explain to any of them what she was doing there, bag-free, in her scrappy wool coat, clutching (later, now) a half-drunk bottle of orange juice and a book marked in places by strips of paper.

Her eyelids drifted down. Sleep! What a good idea. Couldn't she have a brief nap while she waited? Just a little one, darling, as Dorothy Parker might say, just a little one.

Her head dipped down; she jerked it back up in the dull, drooling shock of temporary narcolepsy. Wait! What? Where was she? Had she slept?

"Final boarding call . . ."

And Flannery saw something, or thought she did. A single frame from the movie: black leather jacket disappearing around a corner. Cue chase scene and loud music. She got up in a flurry, knocking over the orange juice, and sprinted after the imaginary jacket. That elusive strip of black leather, she was sure she had seen it: it had woken her, finally, out of her lifelong stupor.

She ran down the ramp, along a corridor, back up another ramp, and up a short flight of stairs. She was always running, these days.

"Where's the New York train?" she hollered at a potato-faced man in a uniform.

"Platform Four. Final boarding—better hurry."

Flannery reached the platform and looked around wildly. Her hair was all over the place, but it was not the time to worry about that. "Anne!" she shouted generally into the November morning, looking up and down the train, because she couldn't think what else to do, and anything like suaveness or dignity had long since passed her by.

It worked, though.

A face appeared at one of the open doors. No, not a face: *the* face, the face she had been looking for since before dawn, had been seeing all that long writing night whenever she allowed her eyes for a moment to close. That face. Which, unfortunately, looked more bewildered than charmed, right now.

"Flannery! Are you taking this train?" She seemed to find the idea alarming.

"No, no." Flannery ran up to her, holding out the book. "I just wanted to give you this. For your trip."

She knew she must look scattered and unkempt—maybe even a little crazy. She'd hardly slept. But she didn't care now. Her single overriding goal had been to get this bookmarked book to Anne before she left, and she'd done that, and now the rest didn't matter and she could relax.

Anne read the cover. "Jamaica Kincaid! That's very sweet. Thank you."

The potato-faced man blew his whistle. The episode continued cinematic. Anne might have been leaving for the front; Flannery would be playing her bereft, worried sweetheart.

"Well. Have a good Thanksgiving," Flannery said, helpless now to offer anything but anticlimax.

"Yes. You, too. Thanks for the book."

"You're welcome. I hope you like it."

And before Flannery could extend the awkwardness any further, as she no doubt would have, she made herself turn away, with an embarrassed little wave—failing even to register the last expression on Anne's face. Which, if she'd seen it, might have struck her as not unlike longing.

Flannery walked down the steps, slowly, without a backward look. As she made her way back through the station, she realized she had a snow of doughnut sugar all down the front of her jacket. She tried dusting it off with a weak hand. It was impossible not to laugh.

"You're a charmer, Flannery," she said aloud, shaking her head. "I don't see how anyone could possibly resist you."

All she wanted to do afterward was get everything organized, then go to sleep. For weeks, preferably. Flannery had so much sleeping to do. It was very serious. It felt like a job: I've got to clear my desk here, get all these trivial matters out of the way, so I can get to the real task at hand, which is to get some *sleep*.

The organizational matters were fairly painless because she couldn't find Nick and had to leave him a note. (She didn't look as hard as she might have.) On returning to her room after her trip to the station she had found his scrawl of the night before:

JANSEN: WHERE ARE YOU? THE BRAINLESS COMEDY WON'T
BE THE SAME WITHOUT YOU. I'LL TRY TO REMEMBER THE
BEST JOKES AND RETELL THEM TO YOU FETCHINGLY.

Guiltily, she left a letter under his door to say she'd decided she was going to Mary-Beth's for Thanksgiving, because she'd been so kind to ask Flannery, and it would be such a good opportunity for roommate bonding.

AND ISN'T THAT WHAT THESE BRIGHT COLLEGE YEARS ARE
SUPPOSED TO BE ABOUT—FORMING LIFELONG BONDS WITH

Freshman flippancy seemed like a safe way to take shelter.

All that was then left was to tell Mary-Beth herself, which Flannery did as soon as her roommate returned from wherever the medicine people went when they were off duty. She looked slightly nonplussed by Flannery's greeting, but was well brought up enough to pretend she was delighted with the decision. She gave Flannery the address and told her she would be welcome to stay for as long as she wanted—just to let the family know. The meal always started at three o'clock.

Flannery was grateful, then told Mary-Beth that she'd pulled an all-nighter the night before, as if on some heroic academic project, and that she had to crash. So she did. Heavily. It was the first of many long-overdue re-encounters with her dreams.

When she woke up in a drugged state, late afternoon, there was a note left under the door in an envelope marked with her name.

SEEMED INDISCREET TO LEAVE THIS ON YOUR DOOR. ONE QUICK PRE-HOLIDAY TIP: HER NAME IS MARY-JO, NOT MARY-BETH. IT MIGHT MAKE THE BONDING THING EASIER IF YOU GET THAT RIGHT. — NICK

And the embarrassing thing was, it was true.

The campus was quiet as ash, and the leaves had all long since fallen.

Flannery had the place all to herself: the sullen underground library; the flattened, frostbitten lawns; the tiled halls and granite bathrooms, from which the food-worried girls had finally fled, leaving Flannery the lush joy of uninterrupted showers. She even went to the Doodle, knowing it would be free now of its once dangerous diner. Flannery ordered a toasted corn muffin and a cup of coffee. The waitress was rude to her, but not quite as rude as before, and it didn't bother Flannery so much anymore. She flung a sentence in Flannery's direction about being one of the last left to hold out that made Flannery briefly proud, like a pioneer.

There were a few other abandoned souls wandering the barren, purgatorylike landscape, but they tended to avoid each other instinctively, as if they might contaminate one another with their outcast status. Some were legitimate folk, professors or grad students, but she recognized undergraduates, too. Flannery found herself suspicious, wondering, What are you doing here? Don't people like you? Don't you have anywhere to go?—which made her realize they must wonder the same about her.

It was the emptiness, after so much fullness, that Flannery cherished. She had been so overstuffed these months. Impressions and changes and newnesses were leaking out of her all over—there just wasn't *room* in her for all of them. Even from the glowing heart of everything—from the untouchably hot place of her thoughts about Anne—Flannery felt the relief of a vacation. She had done the best she could do: she had written words for Anne. That was all she had. Now she could settle back into herself, and her private dreams, and sleep.

When the phone rang one day, Flannery was startled. She was unsure who it might be, and also whether, wrapped as she now was in solitude, she'd still know how to speak.

"Hello?" Her voice was rusty.

"Flannery?"

"Yes."

"It's Anne. I've been trying to reach you."

"Oh."

She gripped the phone tightly, close to her ear. "Hi. What's up?" As if nothing had happened. As if she'd written not a line. As if she were an innocent spinster, padding around her quiet rooms alone, doing the occasional bit of flowered embroidery.

"I think you'd better come to New York."

Flannery did not know New York except as a movie and a myth. And as a mysterious, emphatic address on nighttime TV ads, when you were asked to send your checks and orders to New York, New York, the repetition reminding you that you were nowhere, obviously, and everyone who was anyone was in New York. *New York*. As if you were too stupid to have gotten it the first time.

On her way to college a few months earlier—in the old days, when she was still a dumb youngster—Flannery had encountered the city only in the chaos of its airport, in a red-eye glare of post-flight bleariness, when she was moving through a bewildering stagger of accents and languages. She was looking for a bus service enigmatically called a "limo," which connoted images of sleek, dark-windowed cars, when all it turned out to refer to was a big blue van and an irascible driver, who threw her bags into the back before speeding her and a half-dozen sleepy others to a state she'd heard of, vaguely, but had never quite been able to spell.

The train she rode now was an overlit jostle of tabloid readers and hunched watchers through the grimy windows, and the occasional late, pinstriped commuter with a neatly folded *New York Times*. Flannery had books with her, of course, but her nerves were too raw for her to open them, and she couldn't stop looking everywhere around her, staring at the faces, searching the colorless blighted stops en route for anything like the glory and glamour she'd imagined.

She never did see it. Flannery didn't even recognize the city as the train approached it. It was not as though the Statue of Liberty waved you in with her welcoming torch (like those bright-batoned men at the airport) — or that Flannery would recognize the Empire State Building, for example, if it was right in front of her. Perhaps it was; she certainly saw a cluster of high buildings in the distance, but they swiftly disappeared as the train dipped into a rancid tunnel, when the standing and coat-donning of those around her tipped her off that they were nearly there.

The train stopped with a shudder. People gathered their bags and proceeded to hurry one another onto the platform.

Flannery, imitating everyone carefully, did the same, following the crowd out to the station. Maybe, if she could stay a little longer among their New York numbers, no one would have to know that she was not, actually, one of them.

"What are you reading?"

A touch on her shoulder and Flannery forgot the many ignominies of the morning that had nearly derailed her. A touch on her shoulder and she turned to discover Anne—more vivid, alive, and striking than she had been in Flannery's grainy reimaginings. It always seemed to be this way: there was always more perfection there, in that single person, than Flannery could realistically recall.

"Oh—just this," she said, closing her book to show the cover of a volume of Julio Cortázar's stories. As if she hadn't spent half an hour choosing which title to display, one that might have the right combination of seriousness and surprise.

"Julio Cortázar?" An excited intelligence brought Anne's features into even sharper focus. It was the right choice. "He's fabulous. So eerie. But also humane. He was a big translator of Poe, you know."

"The professor said he only just died."

"Yes." Anne stroked the cover with her fingers, as if to remind herself how the stories felt. "Let me guess. World Fiction?"

Flannery nodded, and they spoke, with the eagerness of readers, of fictional worlds—Cortázar's and Kincaid's and others'. Flannery's thoughts and words already felt more rapid here.

They had just launched right in, breathlessly, before Anne had ordered or unzipped. Eventually she did both, and pulled out her cigarettes.

"So," she said, lighting one, "you found this place okay?"

"No problem." Flannery had allowed herself over an hour to get from the train station to the café in the Village whose address Anne had casually suggested on the phone—"MacDougal, between Washington Square and Bleecker. All right?" Flannery had needed every excruciating minute of that hour in order to submit to a fiasco of misunderstood subway maps, clambering out at a stop many long blocks away, and finally, in a panic, getting into a cab for what turned out to be a two-minute drive to her destination.

"You know," Flannery said, trying not to sound shy or stupid, "it's great to be here. I've never been here before."

"To New York? Never?"

"Nope."

"Really?" Anne laughed. But it was a laugh of invitation, not a shutting out. "My God. Then what are we doing here?" She stood right back up again, without waiting for her espresso. She stubbed out her cigarette with a blunt impatience. "Come on! Let's go."

Everything was so tall in New York that Flannery felt insignificant. She'd always known she was insignificant, of course, but she'd never had the point made quite so graphically before. The buildings and noise dwarfed her, and the swerving, loud traffic made her shrink. Anne, on the other hand—small, intricately formed Anne, whom Flannery knew she could contain in her arms, could carry over any threshold they might cross together—seemed suddenly bigger.

"This is the only city in the world," Anne said, her voice fluorescent, her eyes hectic with joy. In her tight black leather jacket and her black jeans, she was clothed right along with the crowd. "It's the city all the other ones secretly want to be. It's the one all the others chase after."

Like you, Flannery thought, but all she said was, "You're bigger here."

"Everyone is."

"No." Flannery shook her head. "I'm not."

Anne stretched in the sun-slanted street. They were walking down Broadway toward Houston, and the early light reached them in a way that made each step important. Everything was anointed by the light: the bored pretzel seller, the homeless shuffler, the graffiti-blasted subway sign. Storefronts opening with a clatter to begin their day selling music or jackets, used books or vitamins, camping gear or Italian sweaters. And two women, one older, one younger, making their boot-and-shoed way along the great, grimy sidewalk.

"Even you, Flannery," Anne said, and there was a keenness, an edge in her voice that gave the student hope suddenly. It was not the edge of instruction or sarcasm: it was an edge that might cut into some different heart altogether. Flannery heard it. She listened carefully.

"—If only you knew it."

Not long after, they stopped at a dank vacant lot near Prince Street, where stalls clustered together selling scarves and T-shirts, earrings and incense.

"I want to buy you something," Anne said. "I want to buy you a present."

"For me?" Flannery said stupidly.

"Don't blush, for God's sake. You and your blushing—you're like some Victorian maiden."

It was more the tone Flannery was used to from her, but still there was an intimacy in it that caught at Flannery's throat. She'd noticed her blushing! Wasn't that a kind of compliment? And the word "maiden" hummed in her ears, thrilling her with its mysterious erotic import.

"Well, you act like some stern Victorian mistress. No wonder I blush."

The boldness of the reply made Anne pause to look at her with a raised brow and a slight upturning of the pretty corners of her mouth.

"See? Now you're blushing, too."

"I am not."

Anne found the stall she was looking for. Sunglasses, apparently. She looked at a selection of different styles, from sleazy drug dealer to minimal Lennon, retro cat's-eyes or cool oval blue. Each kind she placed on Flannery's head, then stood back from her, holding her shoulders, watching her intently. Scrutinizing. Assessing. Flannery would certainly have blushed under this attention ordinarily, but she was enjoying herself too much to now. Finally Anne chose a pair to her liking. She turned Flannery around to give her an instant's reflection in one of the tiny mirrors, but it was clear there would be no debate about it, as Anne was already paying the Chinese man for them. In fact, as Flannery looked at herself in the mirror, she didn't quite recognize herself. She liked that.

"Sunglasses? In autumn?" she said, starting to fold them up and put them in her pocket as they walked away.

"Keep them on! Christ. That's the whole point." Anne tapped her lightly. Affectionately, it seemed to Flannery. "Your eyes keep wandering around wildly, as if you were from some tiny one-horse town and had never been to a city before. You'll be safer if you keep them on. Then no one will know how young and innocent you are."

"Oh." It was an insult, obviously, but Flannery smiled anyway. She felt sharp in her new shades. Anne had chosen for her a slickly chic look.

"No one, that is, except me."

To be in this city alongside this woman was an airy exhilaration for Flannery. It was like flying. It was the story you tell your wakeful self before sleep, sure it will never take on the full, lit shape of reality.

In her sunglasses Flannery could look around her with impunity at the diverse, infinite faces; at the blurred jostlings and fast-chattering hawkers and random, optimistic runners; at the rampant signs and signals that competed boisterously against the fundamental drabbery of the city's miles of stone. None of it bore any relation to the collective life in the cities she knew at home. She was here without reference. Often she did not understand what she was looking at. There were pages and pages of books that had turned this city into dazzling fiction, some Flannery had read and many more that she would read through her future. But for now, open and ignorant, she let Anne be the author of what she saw, and the muse for what she would later re-create.

Anne knew the city the way you do a lover, and she had a lover's indulgence, a way of seeing charm and fancy where there was ostensibly none. As they walked, she pointed out buildings to Flannery that had a history public ("Auden used to live on this street, and he'd go buy the newspaper in his slippers") or private ("I was once kissed goodbye on that corner by a friend who died the following week, in an accident"). Anne showed her sudden surprising gardens and the great shape of the grid, recited the many names of innumerable foods. When Anne learned that Flannery did not know what a knish was, she took Flannery east and easter to Yonah Schimmel's Bakery so Flannery could sample a spinach-heavy treat and absorb a crucial fact about how the city tasted. "It's something you have to know," she told Flannery, and "It's okay—you can take off your sunglasses now, to eat."

It was hard, as the hours and light eventually faded, and this wandering dream day passed, for Flannery to know whether she was seeing New York or seeing Anne; whether she was hearing New York's busy commentary or just listening to Anne's. The voice that had serenaded her through the turbulent displaced weeks at college was now walking beside her, shaping the air in her ear, coming resonantly from a nearby body that Flannery wanted to hold. Had been longing to hold. Had written about longing for . . . Those bold words that had acted as a spell, as she'd hoped, to bring the two of them together.

It was a miracle. How was it possible? And more to the point, when would this amiable preamble end?

Dark fell, early, and brought with it a quiet off-set by the luminous neon and the city's waking up for its most famous hours. As New York grew louder, the two grew quieter; the conversation changed and lost something of its earlier energy.

They ate dinner in a Japanese restaurant near Astor Place, where Flannery had the best of both worlds: declining, herself, to have sushi, knowing perfectly well she'd dribble rice and raw fish all down her if she did; but given the rare chance to watch Anne as she placed slithery eel delicately into her mouth and fed herself morsel after morsel of skin-pink ginger. They drank sake and ate eagerly, but the speech between them was uneven.

Ordinary biography did not move Anne, and she seemed happy to let silences break over them like waves. She was scarcely interested in where Flannery was from, or what it was like, or how foreign she felt here, or what that was like. She had obviously not taken in whether Flannery had siblings. (She didn't.) She made one or two references to her own sister, Patricia, who was married and lived in Texas. When Flannery ventured, "What part of New York are you from?"—as if she would have understood the answer, anyway—Anne said in a bored tone,

"I'm not from New York. I'm from Detroit."

"Really?" It was so different from what Flannery had imagined, from the way Anne moved through these streets. Flannery thought Anne must have known them since girlhood. She was sure they'd wrapped themselves around their Anne for years. Now she understood that Anne's adoration was that of the adopted daughter rather than the natural offspring. "So—" Flannery started, eager to know everything. What was Detroit like? How and when had she left it? What—where *was* Detroit, anyway? (Other than in Michigan.) And how had it colored her?

"So." Anne repeated it as a challenge, a taunt almost. She had a steel in her that suddenly appeared at times, closing all the doors, shutting everything down, forbidding absolutely any further questions. It was like a high-tech Bond trick, a foreign locking mechanism: it became abruptly impossible to find anything like an opening.

"Do you miss it?" Flannery asked, thinking how much she missed her own home.

"Almost never."

That was the end of that, quite clearly.

Possibly one day Flannery would learn a little about the "almost." In the meantime, the easiest subject for them to circle back to was reading.

They walked along the street, separate in the numbing November cold, and Flannery sensed that the fire between them—she was sure she'd felt it, once, that she had not invented it—was all but out.

"Where are you staying?"

It was not a question Flannery had fixed an answer to. Not that she'd assumed . . . She hadn't, exactly. It was just that her planning mind had given out past the point where she found the café on MacDougal; if she could just find the café, she thought, the rest—whatever rest there might be—would take care of itself.

"Well, I—I could go to Mary-Jo's. She said I'd be welcome. Or—I can always just take the train back tonight. There's probably one back, still."

"The last one's in about half an hour," Anne said crisply.

Flannery shrugged. For the first time, perhaps, since arriving in New York. But suddenly she was tired. "That's probably what I should do." Her voice was flat. "Take the last train."

They walked in silence. Not an especially companionable one. Flannery was moping; Anne, evidently, was thinking.

"I'd invite you to stay where I am," she said with a trace of apology, "at my friend Jennifer's. But it's such a poky little apartment. It's just a one-bedroom. With a futon." She slicked her hair back behind her ear. "Though Jennifer did tell me the place has a Murphy bed, too. I've never actually tried it."

"What's a Murphy bed?"

"What *is* one?" Anne's tongue was still sharp, though she tried to blunt it somewhat. "You know, you're cute, Flannery—you really don't know a damn thing."

Flannery took hold of Anne's arm then, to slow her down. She was walking so fast! "You've got to stop saying that." She had Anne's attention now. "I know all kinds of things. I know how to survive dorm life, though it's totally degrading. I know how to take the train to New York. And I know how to wait at the train station for someone who's going to New York, so I can give them something I want them to have."

It was the first time either of them had mentioned what Flannery had written. *Pages for You*. Remember?

It broke through whatever carapace had formed over the baffling object of Flannery's desire. "You're right," Anne said. Quietly. "You do know things. I'm sorry, I'm being a shrew."

They were walking down University Place now, and reached Tenth Street. Anne steered them around the corner, down half a block, then stopped. She blew on her bare hands, glanced up at a dim apartment building, kept her eyes away from Flannery's.

"Well, this is it."

Flannery was bewildered. This was what? Goodbye—just like that? Wasn't Anne even going to help her get a cab? Before she could question her, Anne carried on.

"Do you want to come up?" she asked, in an oddly humble voice that just about made Flannery melt right there on the sidewalk. "You can see what a Murphy bed is. It's something every girl, sometime in her life, should find out."

88

It was the flutter-doubt that gave Flannery assurance. As they shed the night's cold, standing in the stuffy intimacy of the elevator, Flannery saw Anne's slight frame shiver—from some hesitation, some internal query. Sensing it, Flannery suddenly knew.

This night is mine. She is giving it to me.

This beautiful confidence kept the young woman cheerful as the older one fumbled with the lock and issued coughed apologies for the paper-strewn disarray of the apartment (but they were formal, not genuine, Flannery thought, and she could see signs, too, of an order in the narrow room, a just in case, for company, clearing). Flannery watched Anne's hands fly about the room untamed, gesturing at Jennifer's Frida Kahlo postcards, her shrine to Marlene Dietrich, the "view" that could be seen, if you twisted yourself around by the window, of Wall Street (but showing this required Anne to lead Flannery over to that end where the futon lay and perform an awkward dance step around an object that said loudly, Bed. *Bed.* BED). Tucked rustily into the wall behind a flamboyant Indonesian print, Anne said easily, on surer ground here, was the Murphy bed. This was a less fraught demonstration, as it implied their sleeping separately, so Anne could show Flannery the lethal-appearing spring mechanism, make an unavoidable joke about the prospect of its giving way, mid-sleep, to snap the sleeper wallward. She patted the traplike item almost affectionately, as if it were a pet.

"Now you know. A Murphy bed. That's how it works."

Then she stood, still jacketed, arms folded, her eyes green as motel-sign neon. Vacancy or no vacancy? Flannery wondered, though she was pretty sure she knew.

"Anne," she said softly. Naming her, she thought, might steady her. Flannery felt protective. "Thank you. For letting me stay." She let the love leak into her voice, hoping it wouldn't frighten her.

"Well. Thank you," Anne replied, with an angled smile directed somewhere at the ceiling, "for writing that poem."

An awkwardness threatened to yawn between them.

"I wouldn't mind—"

"Do you want—"

They both stuttered, stopped, laughed a little at the broken ice.

"—something to drink?"

So they moved to the safer-seeming kitchen, where they sat down at the round table and talked to each other in fond voices, the scattered chat of new friends; while the air around them wondered if they'd soon be more.

There, across the Formica surface, their hands met, Flannery's right to Anne's left: the bodies' first admission that they wanted each other. It was not planned or spoken. It was Flannery seeing those finely shaped, shy fingers, and there is that strange way hands are alive, and animal, separately expressive from the rest of the self. It is no surprise that hands create the characters of the puppeteer, or that movies have imagined them moving independently, spiderlike, around a room. Flannery saw this lovely creature and greeted it with her own, stroking it, covering it, and then, finally, holding it in a half-clasp. A declaration. *I am here. We have touched.*

Anne was quiet. Looking down. Her eyes would not find Flannery's, but her hand held hers, too, returned the embrace with its own strength, so that Flannery knew that Anne was with her, though she was sheltering in some wordless privacy.

Flannery allowed the hands and silence to continue as long as she humanly could, until her nervous heart was stretched taut, too taut to breathe.

"Anne?" she said finally.

The question was everything. It was, in fact, the only question. To Flannery's surprise, when Anne looked up at last to answer it, her eyes seemed darker. With lust, and with something else, too—like grief. Or doubt. She didn't say anything, but she nodded.

Flannery took that as her *yes*. It was her thumb she moved across Anne's mouth then. Slowly. Following the curve of her lips up to that sweet peak, and back down the gentle slope of the other side. Flannery knew that she knew this mouth already, had lived with its shape and its sounds in her imagination, but she had not yet felt it. Her blunt thumb made this first intimate acquaintance.

"You have the most beautiful mouth," Flannery said to Anne. And then she did what she had been wanting to do her entire life.

She kissed her.

You see, it didn't have to be in the dark, after all. It could start in the light. There would be hours of darkness later, sure, when in the moon-cast blue they'd wander over and over this new terrain, learning the lay of the land as much by touch as by sight. There would be that long nighttime, enjoying the obscurity of being in each other's arms. But here was the revelation: it could start in the light. Those uncounted hours alone in her sleepless room had taught Flannery something, after all. That, in love, she could face illumination.

They kissed in the lit kitchen first, because that's where they'd come modestly, just to talk, to sip some small, late tea together. Not alcohol: they had both decided not to drink. They knew they wanted wakefulness, even if neither might have admitted that she knew what for.

The kitchen can in its way be the place for kisses. It is the heart of a home. (Even of a cramped and somewhat neglected fourth-floor apartment.) Flannery did not yet know Anne cooked, but she could see that Anne's body was looser in here than when they'd moved around the bedroom. She seemed to feel freer in this room with the food. The kitchen is, after all, the place of heat and eating; the place of treats for the palate; the place a person comes to first thing in the morning, to read, and wake up, and taste the day.

It was the night they tasted. And each other. Starting slow, and slowly faster, their mouths met: first polite and refined; then affectionate, curious; and finally, as their tongues wandered and hungered, their mouths became wide and their desires wider, and they began to find each other with an urgency that brought to mind the word "devouring." Hands moved through hair coppery and fair, and gradually their bodies drew closer, a chair was moved, the table pushed back. Yet still there was a kind of demureness, almost, a riding sidesaddle, with their legs adjacent, until finally Flannery just climbed off her own chair and straddled Anne on hers, leaning into her, gripping her with her thighs and feeling through their two pairs of jeans the heat now, and wetness.

They kissed like that, through clothes and shudderings, in a light bright enough to capture the startled lust on each other's faces, to watch each other grow mussed and wild, and finally to see, clearly, that they were going to have to go somewhere else, away from the kitchen, where their skins could touch.

PART TWO

It was a lake-blue sky through the window, filled only with the low sound of lovebirds.

Sweet husky calls, a cooing almost, a pleasure-chuckle, some creatures' shared mutual delight. And it wasn't their sounds now. (It might have been, earlier: it would be again, later.) Flannery watched the empty, colored air through the rectangular pane and savored this sung-over spell by herself, the figure lying next to her still heavy with sleep, now quiet, her gifts dormant, her sweet mouth slightly open, exhaling dreams. Flannery watched this sky alone for a minute, seeing for the first time how the world changed after a passionate night. The light, the taste on the tongue, the speed of her mind: all different.

She was not now and would never again be the same Flannery. These unearthly noises from overhead seemed themselves a kind of rechristening, a way of calling her by another name. She was changed, and they told her so.

"I used to think it was the neighbors," said a sleepy voice near her. Flannery shivered in her new skin with surprise. It was the voice of her lover.

"You're awake." Flannery felt suddenly a vast and overwhelming shyness—a panic almost, that she was here, exposed, with this woman she hardly knew, with a woman whose delicious body she

97

had explored, certainly, thrillingly, in the dark, but whom she hardly knew. She was here half-naked with a stranger, Flannery was, with this woman, *with a woman*.

"I thought it was a couple I sometimes see in the elevator when I stay here," Anne went on. "My friend Jennifer calls them the Same Family, because they always wear the same clothes as each other, and they have the same glasses and get similar haircuts. A man and a woman—it's a little strange."

She seemed so awake, though her cheeks were pillow-crumpled and her hair all over. But she told this story as though they were old friends, and Flannery, who had been so startled by the wakened sight of Anne, moved closer now, to listen.

"I always thought that sound was them making love in the morning, every morning, it seemed, with these same cries. I thought, How like the Same Family, to have the same love cries as each other. It's perverse. Finally I mentioned it to Jennifer—just the other night, when she called, to see how everything was going. I said, 'Doesn't that couple upstairs drive you crazy—every morning, with their passion sound track? Like they're trying to let everyone in the building know, We're having sex, folks, and we're loving it!'"

Flannery listened to Anne in wonder. A storyteller! She was a storyteller, too, after all.

"And?" Flannery leaned in closer, to follow the narrative thread. "What did she say—your friend Jennifer?"

Anne's eyes woke up with the joke of her mistake. "She told me it's not the Same Family at all." She laughed. "I felt so stupid. It's the pigeons."

They spent hours, or maybe it was days, in and out of each other's grasps and embraces. Waves would crest, and break, and crest again. Urgencies yielded to the slower breaths of satisfaction, as sticky hands stroked or petted, after: the "There, there" and "How was that?" of the relishing lover. Early on—after they had left the kitchen for their first encounter with the futon they'd come to know so intimately—Flannery had whispered, "I've never done this before," and Anne had whispered back (a hot temptation in Flannery's ear), "You'll be fine: I bet you're a fast learner." It gave Flannery the confidence to believe it was true. As it proved to be. And there were sweet 2 or 3 a.m. encouragements: "Are you sure this is your first time? Well, kid—you're a natural."

They certainly built up an appetite. Noonish the day after their first night, Flannery announced, "I have to eat something soon or I may faint." "I know. I think we've burned through all that Japanese food." Reluctantly they rediscovered the art of dressing themselves and, more entertainingly, each other: slow blue-jeaned zips up to a fastening waist button, the neat fondle of jacket snaps. They found the street, which seemed a loud and lopsided place, but fortunately contained a breakfast and hamburger joint where they could stock up on protein. They watched each other eat with belated bashfulness, finding in the act an echo of what they'd just been up to. "Maybe we should get a few things to go, too" was Flannery's practical suggestion, but the minute she said it she blushed at the implication. "Good idea," answered Anne, licking her lips—whether with lust or to free a bit of ketchup, it was hard to tell. They staggered back to the apartment under the weight of juices, sandwiches, and a few other essentials from the Korean grocery. "I feel like we're going camping." "I know. Do you think we should buy a flashlight? And a box of matches?"

Upstairs again, they'd lounge, then lunge. They rested. They rolled; rocked; wrangled. They arm-wrestled in the kitchen for a while, in a lull. Flannery was stronger than Anne, but only just, and she admired the tautness of Anne's forearms. (She remembered them from that party night by the window.) "Do you work out?" Flannery asked. "No," Anne told her. "It's all the theory I read. Keeps me in shape."

They kitchen-kissed again, then rewarmed the bedroom. Once, sitting up, Flannery gave a startled look at the other wall. "It's eerie," she said. "I feel like there's someone else here, watching us."

"Who, Jennifer? Don't worry about her. She's in Toronto arguing with her family. She won't be back till Saturday. Besides—she'd approve."

"Not Jennifer." Flannery looked doubtful. "I think it must be . . . Murphy."

"Murphy?" Anne pointed at the bed glued discreetly to the wall. It did have an unobtrusive, eavesdropping look about it. "What, you think Murphy's kind of a voyeur—'Two women together, how sexy,' that kind of thing?"

"Not only that"—Flannery gave a cartoonish wink—"I think he wants a piece of the action."

"You know what? I think you're right." Anne narrowed her eyes lasciviously. "And why shouldn't he get some?"

So they unfolded Murphy and had a threesome.

If doubt had smoldered in Anne at first, the sex extinguished it. So Flannery had to assume, since she could recognize the tremble of hesitation in a person, as she had in Anne earlier that first night. (Her shudder in the elevator.) As their love wore on and they wore themselves into it, however, it became clear that any hanging back on Anne's part was over.

But what had been her hesitation's source? Flannery guessed there might be someone else, or the ghost of someone. In such a vibrant life how could there not be? Alive or not (that kisser on the street corner?), present or past (Jennifer, formerly?), Flannery could only wonder. A possibility Flannery glanced at, then turned away from, was a moral qualm about palming a student—might not Anne worry over the propriety, or even advisability, of it? (Flannery was certainly not going to raise that question herself.) Finally, she thought it might be Anne's own newness around another woman, but from how she talked and moved, from brief mentions and quick jokes, that was evidently not the issue.

Then again, maybe Anne's worry had been cruder. Perhaps she had not seen ahead of time, as prescient Flannery had, how synchronized these two might be. She might not have devoted as many dimmed evenings to its imaginings as had Flannery. How could Anne know how this lanky girl might appear, stripped of notebooks and knapsacks and the other protective garb of student-hood? Flannery reminded herself that previously she'd been a shy stutterer in Anne's presence, a drunken near-escapee from a party, an uncool White Russian sipper—a twitchy chipmunk, in short, overeager in offering treats and dates to her beloved. Don't forget you were her pupil once, even if for one session only: back-of-the-class Jansen, doodling inattentively, not answering the questions. After all, you're a kid. Naïve; inexperienced. How attractive is that? Maybe Anne had been expecting fumblery and awkward edges, the embarrassing wince of misplaced digits, those painful touristic questions: "Which way do you . . . ?" "Here? Is this good?" "What? Did you say faster?"

And maybe, in that scenario, her doubt was just doused by the floodwaters of girlish excitement they produced between them. Her questions were silenced by their pleasure calls, and the smooth-ness and fluidity of their limbs together calmed her.

Lying flat, looking at the ceiling, Flannery felt free to talk. This was something else Anne had unlocked in her: her unsuspected wish and ability to speak.

"I never knew this before. I never knew this was possible before." On *this* she pressed the nearest patch of Anne that was to hand—her warm thigh.

"Did the boys leave you cold?"

"No. Not cold, exactly. Lukewarm, maybe. I liked boys. I just never thought . . ?" Flannery's sentence wandered off, unfinished. "How about you?"

"What?"

"You and the boys?"

"Boys? I've had a few." Flannery heard a laugh that came from somewhere else—another city. Another story. "Then again, too few to mention."

"That's not true. You've had more than a few."

Anne pulled away at that. "Why do you say that? How do you know?"

"I just do. I can tell." She did not even bother to argue it. When Flannery spoke in that tone, occasionally (perhaps she'd start using it more now), you could hear the adult in her; the one who was aware of her own intelligence and trusted it. There was no room for contradiction. "But you don't care to mention it."

The ceiling watched the naked girls impassively.

"Well." Finally. In a deliberately casual drawl: "I'm sure you've had a few, too. Even if they left you lukewarm."

"No. I told you." Flannery rolled over now to kiss Anne's shoulder. "You're my first."

"Your first of this gender, I thought you meant."

"Nope. My first of any gender, of any kind."

"My God." Anne gave a small, alarmed laugh. "That's such a responsibility! I had no idea."

"It certainly is." Flannery demanded an embrace from her deflowerer, and got one. She looked at her sternly. "I hope you take it very, very seriously."

"From now on" —Anne cleared her throat— "I certainly will."

So people showered together! That was what went on. Who knew? Flannery, for one, had never foreseen such a thing.

The shower was such a personal space, not somehow unlike the womb, or the confessional. A space not imagined for two. First, because it was a part of that shrine to hygiene, the bathroom—the room where all your unmentionable questions could be asked ("Have I got—?" "Is that a—?" "Where's my—?") and sometimes, in a good light, answered. The room where you did what you could to follow dutifully the rules: floss your teeth, wipe the right way, rinse and repeat. Rinse and repeat. Like most rooms the bathroom contained a unique catalogue of your complex self, the bathroom cabinet, in the same way that the kitchen described you by the contents of your refrigerator, and your living room by the books on your shelves.

Flannery was still recovering from the riotous lack of privacy of the dorm's group bathroom, where you were rarely alone and had to pretend, through regretful, gritted teeth, that the experience was just like *camp*, which could be fun. Couldn't it? Performing your ablutions together with other people, chatting over the toothbrushes, sharing conditioner across the shower divider. Like camp, or the gym, a place Flannery had just started going to swim,

105

where even the body-shy have to shed their inhibitions and learn to wash themselves freely in the bright glare of the public.

But showering *with*. Showering with a lover. What a strange sensation, another of the seemingly unending dimensions of romantic life Flannery had not encountered, even in her hard-working fantasy. Soaping up a lover's body: developing the same fond ease with it you have with your own, with the difference that you love that other body without reservation but are bound to have some quibbles and complaints about the one you were born with. Rubbing the bar under her arms and then over them, across her sleek-boned back and shoulders, working up a slippery lather with your active hands. Taking turns, for fairness, under the hot center of the water stream. Shampooing her hair, massaging the gel into that firm head with your warm fingers.

Rinse and repeat.

Flannery loved it. Luxuriated in it. Was baptized, blinking, by the sheer splashing soap and water of it. Hard not to wonder, as she perpetually did: Why wasn't I told of this before? Why did they keep from me the key fact that this bliss is possible?

And, at the same superstitious time: is this bliss really possible? Is it?

And then there was sleep.

It was not something Flannery had ever spent time imagining: that privatest part of a night spent with someone else. The soft tangle of another body to accompany you as you made your bold and dogged way through your dreams. Surely that was the most secluded, most interior thing, actually, more than this flailing new ecstasy of juices and explorations, all these calls of the wild? Flannery had gotten used to the idea that another person—this cherishment, Anne—had seen her naked, continued to see her bare and to know her, breasts and knees and back and warts and all. The modest, never-skirted, one-piece-rather-than-bikini, turning-her-back-to-the-other-girls-while-she-changed Flannery had gotten used to flaunting it (sometimes) in front of her luscious and appreciative lover.

But *sleeping*: that was a new intimacy altogether, and one Flannery often could not believe she shared. It was a secret, wasn't it? Sleeping? What a person looked like when they couldn't help it; what that defenselessness might suggest; what revelations might be conveyed by that loosened, floppy shape, in the unintended words or murmurs of the dreamer? Flannery did feel, in her gut, that any discoveries one person made about the other while she slept were unfair. It was like cheating on a test. (She'd always been struck by the song about a woman who learns of her lover's infidelities from the endearments he speaks in his sleep.) Flannery felt that who you were when you were out and off the record was nobody's business but your own. She could never believe people allowed themselves to sleep in public, in class or at the library—those sprawled, flattened figures scattered everywhere like battle corpses, collapsed in damp and possibly drooling heaps across their books. Exposed!

To sleep with Anne was, for Flannery, an ultimate trust. It was the handing over, the giving in. It was more than the keys to the realm: it *was* the realm, the realm of the deepest self, and if Flannery was willing to go there in Anne's company, she must be willing to go anywhere with her. Albuquerque, for example, or Paris, or the dark heart of the Everglades.

Their first nights together, Flannery made sure she stayed up past Anne, till she heard her lover's breathing slow and thicken, and she willed herself to wake up earlier. That was how she stayed safe. But, cumulatively, the fewer hours' rest made her tired, and several days along she stayed up late past Anne, only to wake in the morning to find Anne's cat face watching her. Watching her while she slept.

Flannery sat up, startled.

"What? What are you looking at?"

"You. Sleeping."

"Why—" Flannery started to panic. "Why—? What's the—?" before she felt the love break over her like a wave.

"Hush." Anne kissed her. "You're beautiful when you're asleep," she said. "Beautiful."

And Flannery believed her.

Two days into all this love, her muscles sorely stretched, her body shocked and soaking, though somehow, impossibly, wanting more—

Flannery went to Thanksgiving.

She had to. There was only so much rudeness she could allow herself, and Mary-Beth—*Mary-Jo*—had been good enough to invite her. (Anne planned to make a private pumpkin pie for herself and work.) Reluctantly Flannery left behind the thankful gift, her new discovery, and cleared her head for New York company.

They were so nice, and it was such a large, luxurious apartment—it was hard not to notice the difference from the cramped theorist's quarters. All the people had wide smiles and big handshakes, and Flannery could not remember a single name. She was underdressed, she realized immediately, since everyone else looked formal and aristocratic, as if they spent quite a lot of time drinking martinis and eating roasted cashews. Flannery had worn what her mother might charitably have called "slacks" ("Don't worry, honey, those slacks look nice on you"), but the truth was, they were pants, and the other women there were in skirts and dresses. This made Flannery feel immediately visible as a *woman being sexually awakened by ANOTHER WOMAN*—that nasal misfit: a lesbian— but if the word was printed on her forehead, everyone was too polite to mention it. They were all polite altogether: no one stared at her pants, or her short unvarnished nails, or her slush-covered boots (girls wore heels, she learned by example); no one acted horrified when she confessed that she was Undeclared in her major. Mary-Jo had the whole college experience wired, quite clearly, and Flannery could see why. She was following in the footsteps not just of Dr. Dad, a warm, broadcaster-voiced man in orthopedics, but also of Dr. Mom, who was an oncologist—a word that stuck uneasily in the back of Flannery's throat because she couldn't remember what it meant, and it seemed embarrassing to ask.

Public radio; New York City politics; favorite stuffing recipes; the year that Mary-Jo made the pumpkin pie with salt instead of sugar; the president of their university, who according to Dr. Dad was a terrifically funny guy, but who'd have thought he'd nail that job? Such was the talk of the feast as turkey, cranberry sauce, and the other ritual trappings were generously doled out. Flannery spent some time next to a bony woman in red who accepted a sparse plate of turkey (no skin) and just green vegetables, then told Flannery all about her fresh divorce and her daughter, who was spending this holiday with her boyfriend, and how much she missed her.

By nine, stuffed and suffocating, Flannery felt she could decently leave. They asked her to stay, of course, so she had to say, "Oh, I'd love to, thank you, but I'd better get back. I have a lot of work to do." "But, Flannery"—this was Dr. Dad—"are you sure the trains run this late? On Thanksgiving?" "I think I can just make the last one. It goes in about half an hour." Oh, yes. What a New Yorker Flannery pretended to be: as if she knew the timetable by heart. They tried a few more murmuring protests, but Flannery could see they were relieved, too. The woman in red could clearly hardly wait for her to leave, so she could update Mary-Jo's mother on the divorce news.

Mary-Jo's father came down with her after the goodbyes, to help her hail a cab. They waited in the cold for a minute. The streets were peaceful in the overfed aftermath of the holiday.

"So," said Dr. Dad, with a smile in his voice she hadn't heard upstairs. "Rushing back to campus, eh? At this hour?"

"Well, you know. I've got a lot of reading. Some papers due."

"Sure, of course. They load you up with work over the break, I remember that." Mary-Jo's father had gone to the same university—back in the bad old days, he'd laughed when he told her, before they let the pretty girls in.

A cab approached them finally, and Dr. Dad put a protective arm around Flannery as he checked out the driver. "You know where you're going?" he asked her gently.

"Sure—you know—Grand Central," she stuttered.

"Of course." He winked, and gave her a hug goodbye. "Good luck, Flannery. I hope he's a nice fellow. He's lucky to have you."

When do the endearments begin? When does "honey" start, or "sugar," or "babe," or whichever lower-case term seems right to capture the spontaneity of fondness? All those times when a given name seems too formal, too serious or even harsh, and you want something friendlier as a salute or calling.

In their earliest days it was only "you" between them. (The way "Hey, you" can become the tenderest utterance.) It was all they needed. But by the time they left New York, Flannery realized she had become Anne's "babe." "Come on, babe, let's go." "Hey, babe, do you want some coffee?" Flannery liked *babe*. It wasn't too frilly or delicate—it sounded tough, like they were in this together. *It's you and me, babe. I got you, babe.* It made Flannery feel like a rock chick, as she told Anne later; after which she had to, on demand, play a minute of air guitar and toss her blond mane around as any self-respecting rock chick would.

But what could she call Anne? Flannery could not pull off "babe": it wouldn't have sounded authentic, coming from her. She didn't have the jacket for it, or the attitude. Her voice was too faint. (She had never much liked her voice.) *Honey* brought on thoughts of her own mother, a constant *honey*er, which was not a good idea; and *darling* was never even in the running. Which left sweetheart. *Sweetheart.* It seemed to fit. It was a classic, after all, and yes, sweet, without being cloying. She tried it out to see how it sounded.

They were on the train together back from New York. Anne was reading. Flannery had been looking out the window, not seeing the trash-strewn landscape, blinded as she was by the overwhelming fact of how much had happened, how completely the world had changed since she had last ridden this train in the other direction. She turned, and in an unrehearsed voice said,

"Sweetheart?" She cleared her throat. "Could you pass me the newspaper?"

"Sure." Anne hardly looked up from the page to find the paper and hand it over.

"Thanks," Flannery said casually, so that only she knew of the thrilling step she'd just taken.

Flannery had never before had a *sweetheart*. And now she did.

If Anne had been flawless from an untouchable distance, she became sublime, close to. Flannery might have worried—did, in an underlying vein, suspect—that this heroine of hers, this pin-up of smartness and grace, might prove to be clumsy-footed or scarred, pockmarked with some character weakness a young idolizer would not have noticed. Before they'd come together, even stricken as Flannery had been, she could observe her own strickenness and knew that she might have spun this Anne by herself, out of whole cloth. That any actual Anne might be . . . ordinary.

It was not true. The more Flannery knew and saw of Anne, the more she loved her. Her humanness became real: Flannery understood that Anne was brittle-tempered, that she was not always truthful, that she harbored schools of fears under her fearless surface. But these qualities made Flannery want more than ever to protect and adore her—calm her in her tempers, hold her quietly through the stories she did or didn't choose to tell about herself, and especially to life-raft Anne through when the fears gathered round her, threatening attack. Flannery wanted to keep Anne from the airless despair that she knew pulled on her. There were days when she could feel Anne drift toward its temptation.

Meanwhile, as afternoons were given over to taking in her lover's look and movements, she became more fascinated by every curve and crevice, every gesture and hesitation. She knew Anne's face when it had a pale, sleepy sheen, and when her hair was scattered and unkempt. There was a wildness to her beauty then that had intimations of the Brontës. ("You're very wuthering today, sweetheart," Flannery told Anne once, but it was an unsuccessful compliment. "Whom did you have in mind? Cathy or Heathcliff?" "Oh, I hadn't decided. A bit of both." Her former instructor shook her head, unimpressed by the lack of clarity.) Flannery saw her lover as she slowly smartened herself in the mornings, fitting into her close jackets, her dark jeans, those sturdy and delicate boots. She saw her neat body readied for a day's admiration from other people. Because, unlike Flannery, Anne knew she'd get that kind of attention. She groomed herself for it.

Flannery kissed Anne's clothed shoulder, remembering the taste of the skin beneath those layers of wool and leather. She could kiss her everywhere, and did. Her mouth roamed over Anne's body as freely as her hands, and eyes, and words. Her mouth knew that body's secret distinctions: its caches of salt, its various textures (the way her earlobe was soft as dough; the hot fold at the top of her thighs), its hypnotic smoothnesses along her back, her cheeks, her stomach.

But Anne's mouth was still Flannery's favorite place. Her home away from home. Her own went there always, before and after, returning contentedly to the perfectness of a kiss.

Once there, she could stay for days.

And she loved Anne's breasts.

It had nothing to do with being a baby or a mother, though it had everything to do with the thrill of drawing out that hollow call from Anne. When Flannery lay along Anne's lower torso, enjoying her breasts, her hands cupping those beautiful bare shoulders she'd first wanted in Cameron's crowded apartment, she could feel, with each pull of her tongue, the moan move through Anne's body, traveling up, slowly, on a sheer current of pleasure, till it crept up her throat and escaped her helpless lips. Flannery would do anything to provoke that moan. It became her favorite sound in the world. She sometimes felt it was so strong and sinewy that she could have climbed up it, as if it were a rope that could bear her weight. Sometimes as she sucked Anne's breast, till her tongue was all but numb and Anne's nipple some-how changed flavor—Flannery could not have described the change, but she could taste it—she felt she was climbing up that pleasure-call of Anne's, even as she slid back up her body, planting aftermath kisses along her breastbone and soft neck; by her ear; on her cheek; and, hushed conclusion, on her lips, now that they'd stopped groaning and had settled back from gasping into some-thing calmer, like the hum of a dreamer.

Flannery loved Anne's breasts; and Anne, for her part, loved Flannery's love.

"What did you do to me?" she'd ask Flannery, when her lover had returned to face her, after such a passionate mission. "What did you do? I've—I've never felt anything like that before."

Anne's face was bashful, her skin the rose of post-climax, and Flannery was unable to keep from her own a sly smirk. It was her most prideful achievement. It brought on the narrow-eyed arrogance of conquest, followed by a simple, affectionate delight.

"I don't know what I do," she whispered into her lover's mouth. "But whatever it is, I'd like to do more of it."

Did Flannery believe in souls? She wasn't sure. Or spirits, or other ineffables? She was scared to ask Anne her views on the matter, as it might be something Anne would laugh at. Flannery did not want to risk that laughter.

If she did believe in souls (maybe, who knew, it was something she'd have to grow up a little to form an opinion on), she would say that Anne's spoke to her through her eyes. Whatever pleasures their bodies shared, it was Anne's eyes that moved Flannery most deeply. Deeper, certainly, than anyplace words could reach. It made her suspect that eyes must communicate something of the spirit.

She tried, though. She tried to find language to express what she felt.

"Your eyes—"

"They glitter like a cat's—"

"They are filled with some incredible light—"

"Your eyes are so—they're *beautiful*."

Anne watched her struggle, but how could she help her? Flannery searched for words to convey the color: she rummaged around the minerals, coming up with the obvious jade and emerald and, finally, malachite; she said often how feline they were, in color and in that slow, assessing stare. She found the greens outside sometimes, a new bud, a vivid blade of young grass. "There! Look! Your eyes—that color—" But Anne would shake her head, head-tussle her lover, and say, "Stop trying so hard, babe. I know. I get it. You like my eyes."

God, no. It was much more than that, but Flannery would never find a way of saying it. It remained stuck in her throat, what she wanted to speak of how Anne's eyes held the concentrated, bright essence of the person Flannery loved.

Many years later, in London with friends, Flannery would find a color that came close. *Absinthe.* She had never heard of it. Her friends laughed about its mythic strength when they saw a bottle of it in a liquor store window. Flannery, stalled, looked away. She lost herself on that damp street, lost London entirely, as she absorbed that vibrant color, and with it a memory of the unmatched fire of her passion for Anne.

And Flannery, too, was discovered. She learned for the first time that she was beautiful, a notion that had never occurred to her before. In Anne's resonant voice she heard herself described as graceful, lean, curved, lovely—and came to believe the words, a little.

She was learning what it felt like from the inside, this great life secret. She was finding herself capable of sounds and furies she would never have dreamed of—not in *Flannery*, the self she'd known.

Was it like this for everybody? The transformation, and the contrast? Flannery was a still, quiet person: that's how she seemed even to herself, though in her adolescent journal she had recorded rollicking emotional turmoils, and had known herself capable not just of love (unrequited, for a guitarist in a band) but of disappointment, melancholy, dreamy optimism, and soulful, self-important philosophizing.

But not *this*. Never this. Even Anne, who claimed she'd always sensed this fire under the Nordic Jansen calm—"I saw you dance, babe, and I could see it *then*"—even Anne sometimes looked at her hair-swept, sweat-tossed lover and said, her own cheeks hot with surprise, "My God! There's something in you, Flannery. There's something, it's so wild—where does it come from?" Then, to counter the hint of alarm in her voice, she added, "It's wonderful."

Flannery did not know what it was, or where it came from. Did everyone have this? Perhaps not. Did the measure of her passion relate in some way to the measure of her long years of repression? (They felt long to her; and she would soon be eighteen now, which showed just how old she was getting to be.) While all those other kids were playing doctor and nurse and feeling each other up in the cupboards, Flannery Jansen was reading peacefully at home, gathering all her resources for this moment, this intense future adventure with Anne, which would take her into the deepest throes of her shockingly savage body.

It terrified Flannery. Absolutely. She spent nights back in her dorm room blank with fear. What had been released in her? In Anne's company she mostly felt all right about her expressiveness. No, not all right, she felt *exultant*: here she was, a new person, a woman, a sexual explorer bringing delight to the face she loved most in the world.

Alone, back in her room, she lost her confidence. Quiet again, the way she had always been before, the way she had known herself best, Flannery would sometimes feel completely, darkly convinced.

This can't possibly be me.

And:

I've got to get out of here.

They tried to get back to work. It was something they both had to do as December uncoiled, snakelike, toward finals—and, worse, MLA. Anne was not only giving her paper there, she was going to be interviewed for academic jobs. Anxiety frequently threatened her like an angry swarm of bees.

Together, in Anne's living room, which was also her bedroom, which was not altogether separate from her kitchen, they tried to work. Far from seeming cramped or enclosed, the room was open, spacious, full of light and novelty and the echoes of what they had done there. The walls were white. The angles were modern. A skylight slanted along the sloped ceiling, and Anne had arranged her bed so that the window's trapezoid of winter sun fell on her bedspread. She lay on her side within that clutch of light, reading, head cradled in her eloquent hand. That hand: it was hard sometimes for Flannery to look at it without remembering its other talents.

"I can't concentrate," she said. She was sitting against a wall in the corner near two heaps of books: a pile for Revolution, for which she'd chosen to write about China, and a pile for Criticism, for which she'd chosen to write about Susan Sontag. Neither could hope to compete with the temptation of watching Anne read.

"Try." Anne didn't even look up.

A book spread across her knees, her head dipped misleadingly down. Flannery sneakily stared over at Anne on the bed. Those smart eyes (she could only glimpse the green) covering yards of words, translating all those ideas, moving in and out of real and imagined territories with confidence. The way Anne read was like the way she stepped down the street: sure of her carriage and her direction, while staying open to the new colors and languages around her. It was how Flannery had loved her first, after all. Then, as now, reading through some world that Flannery couldn't even see. The title of the book was hidden.

"You know, I could spend my life watching you read."

Anne pursed her lips. "That would be tiresome."

"For you, maybe. Not for me. For me, it would be heaven."

This made Anne's eyes flicker away from the page. Reluctantly. She did not want to be interrupted right now.

"Flannery," she said slowly, unable to resist entirely the sound of the name in her mouth, "don't you have work to do? Haven't you got a paper to write?"

Flannery took her eyes away from where they wanted to be and returned them, dutifully, to the arguments of Susan Sontag.

"Yes," she said forlornly. In a voice heavy with the wretched melancholy of frustration. "I guess I do."

Flannery only ever wanted to speak poems, unforgettable lyrics, about her nights (and days and mornings) with Anne. That time was sublime. Of course. Yet sometimes, prosaic girl that she more naturally was, she had to accept a blunt fact, too, of her Anne hours: that, at a certain technical level, she was getting the how-to.

One December evening in the dining hall Flannery overheard a conversation fragment from a neighboring table. Crew types, more or less, looking at a flyer advertising a Gay and Lesbian dance and making cracks about gay sex. "Hey, it's got to give you a serious advantage," ventured a bulky, joky guy, "to know the equipment so well in the first place. I mean, think about it: you're already a licensed driver." But that was the whole point, Flannery wanted to lean over and tell him. She wasn't a licensed driver at all—she'd just gotten her learner's permit. She was still more comfortable in the lower gears and would not yet have considered herself safe for freeway driving.

She learned about herself by learning Anne. And as Anne explored her, she brought to life parts of Flannery she had never conceived of and couldn't have begun to name. Once, Anne had found a spot within Flannery that seemed to be the single concentration of her excitement. It was the place of pleasure, purely, and when it was touched, Flannery just flooded with delight. Literally. As though Anne had turned on a tap. Flannery would have been embarrassed, if she hadn't been so high on the sensation of it. Besides, Anne herself was crowing with the discovery.

Later, when Flannery had recovered and come back to the ground after her free flight, she wanted to return the favor. She searched, with clever fingers; and she was rewarded. *Gold*. Eureka! Flannery was as proud as any pioneering forty-niner.

Afterward Anne, as stunned as Flannery had been, panted her thanks.

"Well," Flannery said modestly, "I had to try to do what you'd done. It felt—it felt so good." When Anne laughed at that, Flannery said nervously, "What's so funny?" She was too sensitive yet to take teasing about her lovemaking. "What?"

"No, I'm sorry. I was just thinking. Of what they say." Anne smiled, then winced with apology. "You know—how imitation is the sincerest form of Flannery."

There were other games Anne played with her name. "Flannery will get you nowhere" became a common currency between them: Anne said it to herself in Flannery's presence, when she felt she wasn't getting enough work done—when their love and lovemaking were distracting her from what she only half-jokingly called her higher purpose. On a good day, when Anne was teasable, Flannery would counter with a touch, and a correction. "Oh no. Flannery will get you *everywhere.*" On a dour day, when the job search worry made Anne's limbs go rigid, Flannery didn't try it.

Another time Anne called her "my *flâneur,*" affectionately, "or my *flâneuse,* I should say."

"What's that?"

"*Flâneur.* It's someone who strolled up and down the boulevards of Paris watching the life of the city. Benjamin writes about them. From Baudelaire."

"I've never been to Paris."

"Really?" It was kind of Anne to act as though the fact weren't obvious.

"*Flâneur.* I like that. It sounds a bit like 'Flannel,' which is what my mother used to call me when I was a kid. When she was

126

trying to get me to go to sleep at night. She called me her little Flannel and held me close to her, pretending I was a blanket."

But Anne never seemed to enjoy these memories. She had yet to evince any interest in Flannery's mother whatever. Competition? Flannery sometimes wondered. Or just a pocket of indifference?

"*Flâneur.* Benjamin writes about it in *Reflections*. He's great, you've got to read him. I can't believe Bradley didn't put him on the syllabus. I'll lend it to you."

"Thanks," Flannery said without enthusiasm. The stack on her dorm room desk of Anne-required reading was growing steadily higher. It discouraged her. She sighed. "I don't think I'll ever catch up."

"It's not a race, you know," Anne said gently.

"Oh. Isn't it?" Flannery went back to her reading. Humming under her breath a childish song her mother used to sing to her, about the Flannel.

Flannery, for her part, was first and most easily tempted by "Annery," though she also tried "Flanne," which eventually mutated, in a jealous moment, to Phil-Anderer, when she felt Anne was keeping from her the important stories about her past.

"Anne the Philanderer," she said in a mock tolerant tone. "I know all about it already. I just wish you'd have the courage to tell me yourself."

"As opposed to your hearing about it from everyone else?" Anne's face was puckered up with a wry expression. No one, as far as either of them knew, had any idea about Flannery and Anne. They shared an uneasy assumption that it might be dangerous if anyone did.

"God, yes. I get so tired of people coming up to me to tell me the stories. 'Anne and Derrida this,' 'Anne and Hélène Cixous that.' Someone claimed they'd seen you arm in arm with Harold Bloom . . ."

Anne's glance flicked out sharply, a sudden switchblade, and Flannery understood she'd taken the joke too far. Bloom was a critic Anne had only acid for, and Flannery wondered if her blind gibe had, inadvertently, landed somewhere true.

Safer, on the subject of their names, was the nice simplicity of the two's relation: "Yours is a subset of mine," as Flannery thought of it; and "Mine is the succinct version: your name, carefully edited," in Anne's formulation. It suited the two of them, they agreed, that Flannery's was the softer and chattier, while Anne's was blunt, direct, and had a 'Get to the point' sound about it. "One syllable, that's all we've got time for," said Anne briskly, clapping her hands like a schoolmistress. "Let's go, let's go. Move along. Saying 'Flannery' can take all day."

One afternoon, when Flannery was trying to wrap her arms all around Anne as she lay curled up fetally on the bed (she was curious to see whether they could reach), Flannery said,

"See? This is how it is. I can contain you here, all of you, right in my arms. The same way my name contains yours. See?"

Anne pulled away. "Contain me? Is that what you want to do?"

Flannery heard the warning, but decided not to let that stop her. "Yes," she said. "My Anne here, where I can always have her."

Anne looked at her then through the eyes of a faint acquaintance. Not unfriendly; just distant, considering. "You know, babe." Her voice had an older woman's weary advice in it. "You're so hungry. You want so much."

"Well." Flannery shrugged. "So what? I'll never get it."

"You might. If you stop asking."

"I'll never stop asking."

"I know." Anne touched her cheek. "It's one of the things that makes you strangely lovable."

December only got darker and sicker, as huddled students with colds staggered around dreading finals and final papers. The library was fluorescently filled with busy notebooks and runny noses. First friendships got consolidated in the crisis mentality of the coming end: end of first semester, end of this grand beginning to Education. Flannery shared term-paper worries with Susan Kim at the bookstore/café; ate Cap'n Crunch with Cheryl one morning, lingering until the dining-hall staff glared at their delinquency. She even went to the ice cream joint with Nick one night. Normally Nick was much too cool for ice cream, but under this intense pressure personalities cracked and people allowed themselves to regress. Over two huge berry and candy bar–scattered scoops Nick said the same thing to Flannery that others had recently said: I hardly see you around anymore. Where have you been hiding? And: You look good—different, somehow. Have you changed your hair? Nick, who had the most immediate reason to have paid attention, seemed to understand that the change was not simply seasonal, that there might be a person behind Flannery's new shape and movement. He had run into the two together once, at the all-night grocery. He was a good guy, though, Nick. What he suspected, he didn't say.

"Take care of yourself, Jansen," he concluded as he scraped rubbery almond pellets from the base of the Styrofoam dish. "Don't burn the candle at both ends. They say it diminishes performance." She eyed him, licking fruits of the forest from a plastic spoon, wondering if he meant the innuendo. He probably did. "Thanks for the tip," she answered, allowing herself an uncharacteristic private query: would this boy, too, have left her lukewarm?

There was, inevitably, a crushing stress that drew closer, the inexorable iceberg, along with the beckoning Christmas break and its promise of freedom. By Christmas Day, Flannery told herself repeatedly, by the time you're eighteen (her birthday crowded around the twenty-fifth), this will all be over. You will have finished your first, shattering semester at college.

She felt the stress. Of course she did. But she was protected from it, too. Wrapped in the arms of her girlfriend—*hers*—Flannery was fundamentally untouchable, even by exams and papers and the grueling needlepoint of footnotes. Whatever letters might collect on her transcript from this first series of professorial assessments, she was not going to panic.

After all, such grades were nothing—invisible ink—next to the permanent imprint she'd wear on her skin from this passion. What marks could matter more than this love's tattoo?

As for the two of them, they had early-winter pleasures to enjoy. Late dawns and early dusks, the sweet taste of smoky kisses when the air outside is iced and salty; the joke of the fifteen-minute striptease, when coats and scarves and sweaters and long johns all have to be shed in a warm floor-bound bundle before flesh can finally meet flesh. Close embraces on late streets, in a lamp-light two female figures (one older, one younger) had to hope would not expose them to unfriendly attentions. Day or night walks through ice-prettified wonderlands, against the ever-present kitsch of carols. Falalalalaing to each other, slyly, in the tinsel-glittered rooms of restaurants or in the naked seclusion of Anne's off-campus apartment, at a safe distance from university eyes.

Each had her own anxiety to inhabit—"You'll do fine," they emptily reassured each other—in a place quite separate from the juicy benevolence of their mutual affection. Anne wrung her hands and devoured cartons of Marlboros at the thought of the MLA ordeal, which would unfold just after Christmas in a fraught, overcrowded Chicago hotel. Sooner than that, Flannery had to walk straight into the source of her panic, somehow to sit in the right rooms at the right times and disgorge all the knowledge she had accumulated of Art History, World Fiction, and

Revolution. For Criticism she wound a long skein of argument around the skunk-haired Susan Sontag; and did not let Anne read the result. They both agreed it was better that way. "I'll have plenty of these to look at soon enough," Anne groused. "The efforts of all your brilliant darling peers." "Give Susan Kim an A," Flannery said. She was brave enough to risk such cracks by now. "Unless you think she's cute, obviously, in which case I think you'd better fail her."

Then the break was on them. Flannery packed for the reverse journey in the blue van with the irascible driver to the chaotic airport and from there west, to home. The dorms were a confusion of suitcases, deadline frenzy, and shouted seasonal greetings. People left before you'd said goodbye to them. Everyone was underslept. There was an escape-from-a-burning-building feel about the place, as students vibrated on their tense diets of caffeine and sugar.

Anne would not do a pre-limo dorm goodbye. She didn't want to say goodbye at all. "It seems overdramatic," she said emphatically. "We'll see each other again in a few weeks. I might be a human being again by then, after MLA. That or a vegetable. One or the other." Anne advised against their spending Flannery's last night there together and thought she'd gotten away with a "See you in a few weeks, babe," parting after a shared spanoko-pita—nourishment that followed a brief and urgent afternoon encounter.

Of course, this meant another short night for exhausted Flannery, who woke to take a dark dawn walk to Anne's apartment. It brought on shadowed memories of her earlier pilgrimage to the train station, for Anne's apartment was on the same route.

An ash-gray, crotchety face appeared at Anne's door; her hair was almost colorless from lack of sleep. But those loved lips did manage a smile when she took in the sight of her up-and-ready, travel-anxious lover.

"You crazy girl," she said affectionately, and opened her arms for an embrace.

"I didn't have time to write you anything this time," Flannery clarified, before stepping in to take up the invitation. "So this is a substitute for a poem." And for the last time in that banner year, she kissed Tuesday Anne, in a long and eloquent farewell linger.

Vacation was an agony of absence.

Her mother was pleased to see her—"I've missed you so *much*, honey," in a fervent hug at the airport—and Flannery suffered a mild guilty heartbreak that the feeling wasn't mutual. There was a deep, primal comfort in being around this familiar life-giving body again, and she did love the harmless trot of her mother's conversation; but she was no longer the essential woman in Flannery's life. She was not the woman Flannery heard when she closed her eyes, or inhaled still in the warm wintry scents of her clothes; she was not the woman Flannery figured as the soft pillow she held close to herself at night, in an empty effort to fill the hollow of her curved, sleeping stomach.

Flannery had never considered that the word "ache" might be meant literally, when applied to the heart. "Heartache" was a fancy, surely, a gift for songwriters and a handy rhyme for "heartbreak." They weren't serious? But no, they were. It was something else to learn. The heart did ache, actually. She felt a dull grind of lack somewhere near her diaphragm, a pain that occupied the space of something removed. A phantom limb. A scratchy hunger. The wasting muscle fatigue of *want*.

Flannery listened and talked with her mother and her friends, and their friends. She told funny stories to these older women, as if she'd just returned from a war. College! What a mad lark it was. She enjoyed these reunions; they were meaningful to her. But she remained separated from her company the whole time by the screen of their ignorance, and her knowledge. They thought—and why shouldn't they?—that this was just Flannery they had in front of them. Same old smart and loping Flannery, sheltered and friendly, cautious and curious, maybe one day a writer. She charmed, in her modest, wise-eyed way. *It would be interesting to see what she'd become.*

It was only Flannery who knew she was already becoming it. It was she who knew that this eighteen-year-old in front of them was someone else entirely. She felt like an elaborate impostor, as if her lines had been carefully rehearsed to sound authentic—the kinds of things Flannery, the girl we used to know, might say.

Christmas Day they spent as usual with her mother's sister's family at a *Better Homes and Gardens* spread of gifts and foods produced by Flannery's shiny hostessy aunt. Sometime after gingerbread and ice cream, Flannery suddenly felt faint with her contained silences and the sharp pain of missing Anne. She couldn't focus anymore on the conversations around her, which had nothing to do with the only person she felt like talking to. She excused herself, saying she had to take a walk.

Her older cousin Rachel joined her. This wasn't part of Flannery's plan. It was solitude she was after, a moment restored to the detailed adorations of her Anne-fixed mind. Now, with coiffed Rachel walking crisp-heeled beside her, more hiding and dissembling would be required.

They walked up the quiet suburban hill, toward the bend from which they could watch the bay. Rachel, not an especially sensitive creature, launched into a complaint about her stuffy parents and from there, seamlessly, into a long account of her college boyfriend, and how freaked out her mother would be if she knew that Rachel had been having sex. Flannery, half-listening, pulled out a packet of Marlboros from inside her down jacket.

"God! Flannery. When did you start smoking?"

"Recently." It was an experimental habit she had just taken up for a specific reason: she wanted to make her mouth taste like Anne's.

"I can't believe it. You've always been so clean-cut."

Flannery nodded noncommittally. Hoping her careless (unpracticed) smoking might put a dent in that image.

"So," said Rachel, suddenly more interested in her younger cousin, who'd always seemed a bit stiff and studious before. "Has college back East turned you into a wild child? A party animal?"

Flannery smiled. "Maybe. A little."

"Do you have a boyfriend out there?"

She looked at the ground. She was a little dizzy; the nicotine made her head spin. "No."

"Really?" Rachel, charitably, looked surprised. "Well, I wouldn't worry about it. You probably will soon. But you know what?" She lowered her voice as if to share an important, helpful confidence. "Maybe you should quit smoking. Guys might find it off-putting—it makes your breath stink."

Flannery coughed and crushed her Marlboro underfoot. She couldn't answer for a minute. Instead, she looked out over the bay's serene spread of water and suppressed a small yelp of help-less longing.

Then, one miracle night, a phone call.

Flannery had given Anne her number and address before leaving, but the mailbox and phone line had so far remained voiceless, so by this late December ringing Flannery had stopped hoping. She sat at the kitchen table paging through the course book, trying to figure out into which new bright fields of literature and ideas the next semester might lead her. Renaissance Poetry? The Age of Enlightenment?

"It's for you, honey. Someone named Anne."

Flannery jumped in her seat, and out of it. "Can I take it—?" she said, reaching for the phone—but there was nowhere else to take it. The bedroom phone was broken, so there was only this one in the kitchen, where her mother sat placidly reading her favorite Jane Austen. Flannery had to wrap herself around the receiver with her whole eager body, in an effort to create a place of her own in which she might enjoy a bodiless reunion with Anne.

"Hello?" She sounded so quiet and tentative, she hated herself for it.

"Hey, babe." The other end of the line had no such hesitation: Anne was there at once, in all her huskily sexy divinity. Flannery leaned into the wall as her knees weakened beneath her.

"Hi," she managed. Hoarsely. "How—how are you?"

"I'm good. How are you?"

"Okay."

"I can hardly hear you." Flannery caught generic crowd noise beyond Anne. Scholars at conference. Ambient bustle. "Here, why don't I close this door and see if that's better," Anne said. The background receded. "So. What have you been doing?"

"Not much. Visiting friends and family mostly. My mother's here, you know, so—"

"I get it. So you can't really talk?"

"Right."

"That's all right. I'll talk for both of us." She lowered her voice. "I've been missing you, babe."

"Me too. I know. Me too."

"They have lovely big beds here at this hotel."

"Really?" Flannery swallowed. "Not here. Here they're—here it's pretty small." She kept her voice peppy and reporterish in case her mother was listening, as she no doubt was. Anne's got even sultrier.

"I've been imagining what we could be doing across it. If you were here."

"Yeah, I know what you mean. Sounds—sounds good."

There was a pause, in which Flannery could hear Anne's heavy breathing. It was a joke, though. Anne laughed. "Is your mother really right there?"

"Yep."

"Well. Give her a kiss for me. Listen." She became brisker. More professorial. "I've got some good news. People seemed to love my Cather paper, and I've got callbacks at two places. NYU, job of my dreams, and—University of New Mexico. I doubt I have a prayer at NYU—it's not really my field. But the New Mexicans seem to love me."

"That's great! God. Congratulations."

"It is pretty good. There are so many morose corpses around here going home empty-handed."

"So. New Mexico. For next year, right?" Flannery's voice became even peppier. Less convincingly. She looked at the serene back of her mother, who was apparently absorbed in Eleanor's big-sister dilemmas. It was *Sense and Sensibility,* for probably the tenth time. "That's pretty far away."

There was a pause, a space of dead air, which Flannery filled completely with the hope that she hadn't wrecked this phone call.

"Flannery?" came an unreadable voice from the other end. "Flannery Jansen? You still there?"

"Yes."

"Good. Because I love you."

Oh. "You too. I mean, me too. That is—"

It was the first time they had said it.

And that made the vacation.

Days later they met up at the Anchor Bar. Anne chose the time and place; Flannery chose her outfit, carefully. An elegant, sea-colored jacket, cut straight and short in a way that complemented her slender height (Rachel had certified it as "nice," a recommendation Flannery hoped was trustworthy), straight Levi's, and a chic new pair of boots, her mother's Christmas present to her, which might now put Flannery's own feet on the map.

Anne was there already, waiting in a booth. The two greeted each other uncertainly in the familiar dim, Glenn Millered interior; not as friends, but not, after this short separation and in the public setting of the bar, as lovers. Not yet, anyway.

Anne had ordered them drinks. Gin-and-tonics for them both—"Because you're a grown-up at last, too, now you're eighteen. You can get married, if you want to. And see R-rated movies by yourself, without an adult to accompany you."

"X-rated, too. Don't forget the Xes."

They sat at the table, unsure how to reacquaint themselves. Anne had an easy prop to hand—her cigarettes. They always gave her a sense of purpose.

Anne was a damn good smoker, and she knew it. Even if she lit up out of concentration or stress, she looked silkily good; but when, as now, she smoked to seduce, she was unmatchable. She took slow drags, slitting her eyes slightly to keep the smoke from watering them, gazing at Flannery, catlike, as she pulled in the necessary nicotine. Her mouth cosseted the cigarette as if it were her long-lost lover; communicated with it privately, as if they were sharing a private joke. It was all Flannery could do not to throw herself across the shot-glass-and-ash-scattered table and submit to Anne's mercy.

Finally she just said it.

"You look so sexy, smoking. You're the sexiest smoker I've ever seen."

Then, because they were in a bar and there wasn't much else she could safely do with her twitching fingers, Flannery reached over to Anne's pack of cigarettes, pulled one out, and lit up. Anne watched her in benign disbelief.

"Is that a cigarette in your hand? Or are you just glad to see me?"

Flannery inhaled, narrowed her eyes, exhaled. Expertly, so she thought.

"Seriously." Anne leaned forward. "Is this your new party trick?"

"I took it up over vacation," Flannery said. "I wanted to taste like you do."

"What—old and ashen?"

"I like it."

"Well, babe." Anne shook her head. "I don't know how to tell you this. But—it doesn't really suit you. You look—cute, you know. Like a kid trying to act grown up."

It was a blow.

"Not very sexy, then," she said morosely.

"Not very. Though—" Anne leaned forward over the bar table, took the cigarette gently from Flannery's fingers, and stubbed it out. Then, holding each of Flannery's hands with her own, she kissed them, one palm after the other. "With your hands free, now *that's* . . ."

Flannery looked around the bar nervously. Such openness seemed risky.

". . . *sexy*," Anne finished in a whisper. Then sat back.

Businesslike now, downing her drink and calling the barmaid over for the check. She packed up her cigarettes and pocketed them. "Yes. That's what we need here," she said. Confident, happy with her decision. "I need you with your hands free, and I need to get you back to my home."

The year's coldest days were the hottest she had ever lived.

They summered inside Anne's apartment with the heat turned high, lounging on the bed as if poolside, sometimes sipping tall, iced lemonades for a joke. Heat was their one, main, luxury: they chose it over dinners out and fancy gifts, or weekend excursions to exotic places. They picked summering in winter as their treat.

Dress code was casual and scant: sleeveless T-shirts and brief white underwear; a blue, long-sleeved man's shirt and nothing else; spaghetti-strap tops, sometimes, on Anne, and calf-length leggings. Flannery's long legs were often free of covering, and she got used to seeing their lean pale shapes stretched out under the admiration of Anne's moving hands. They never wore shoes. Sometimes for days at a time they wore no shoes, and Anne's glorious range of pint-sized footwear remained at a sulky distance from their wearer. Cold-blooded Flannery had to wear socks, even though it was summer, soft comforting blankets for her toes— Anne had laughed with delight for about ten minutes when she first examined Flannery's feet, Flannery never did understand why. Anne was not permitted the same luxury. If Anne covered herself with socks or slippers, Flannery as swiftly removed them, on the insistence that she pet and stroke her, bringing that footloose joy to Anne's face that went along with any attention Flannery ever paid to her precious feet. She kissed them; massaged them; once she even bit them. (Anne didn't like it.) She believed that Anne's feet and her own hands fit perfectly together, and she said so, sometimes. "A match made in heaven." And purring Anne would agree.

As befitted summer afternoons, Anne did sometimes wear sandals around the apartment. They were the only shoes Flannery allowed, because they graced Anne's feet so sensually, decorating them with the shapely leather they cried out for. Flannery watched Anne's feet bathe in her sandals, and she could hardly wait till summer came, when she would be able to hear that satisfying slap against those heels and know that her lover was making her beautiful open-toed way through the world. She dreamed of their real summer-months summer—the one they'd grow warm in together.

Outside, it snowed. And slushed. And froze again; and blackened; and broke bones and sprained ankles, as the treacherous streets caused hurriers to slide, the elderly to fall. Bare branches grew brittle and fractured in the cold snaps, while vicious icicles dangled blades over unsuspecting walkers. There were road accidents and chilblains. Cold sore–blistered lips and encrusted noses. Muffled heads and cloudy speeches, slow-starting cars and the deep-racked coughs of all the stages of bronchitis.

Meanwhile, inside their hot retreat, the two women swooned.

"Look at this. Look at you. You're so *slick*."

"It's sweat."

"I know it's sweat. It makes you shiny. So slippery."

"I'm sorry, I can't help it."

"Don't be sorry!—"

"I've always been a big sweater. I don't know why. I sweat like it's going out of style. I sweat like there's no tomorrow."

"I like it."

"You do?"

"It's sexy. It shows your—eagerness. That you're a hard worker."

"It's not very ladylike."

"Well, no. It's true. You couldn't really call this a 'glow.'"

"I know. There's too much of it for that."

"Mmmm." Anne licked Flannery's stomach clean, slowly, of its thin down of perspiration. Which might have made Flannery ticklish, if it weren't such a good feeling, one she was happy to succumb to. "Salty. Delicious."

"It will make you thirsty," Flannery warned, but she was humming with pleasure.

"If it makes me thirsty," said Anne, "I will go find myself something to drink."

Long and lean was supposed to be the desired shape in life, but next to Anne, Flannery always felt big and gangly. Anne luxuriated over Flannery's legs, running her hands along them as if along a burnished banister. She admired Flannery's height, saying once as an exotic compliment that it made her feel she was dating an elegant Great Dane. "Norwegian," Flannery corrected, not quite sure how to take it.

Despite Anne's graciousness Flannery felt that they both knew that Anne was the one whose dimensions were mysteriously divine. Flannery fit her arm around Anne's neat waist one afternoon, in the languid February heat of the apartment, and told her so.

"You are so small and perfect," Flannery said. "It's just that: you are perfect." She let her hands resculpt Anne's perfection for a soft minute before she heard the silence that met her remark. When she looked up, she found a surprising flutter of grief over Anne's face.

"That," she said, "is almost the precise opposite of what my mother used to say to me."

"Why? What did she say to you?"

"That I was too small. Weak. *Naine*, like my name—it means dwarfish. She didn't like me very much, my mother." Anne

148

laughed. Or rather, made a sound that approximated laughter. "Her life would have been immeasurably better if she'd never had me. She could have left my father and gone back home, to Paris. As she was good enough to tell me, often." Anne reached for her cigarettes from a jumble of torn-off jeans and socks, hunted around for a bedside lighter. Lit, inhaled, plucked a piece of tobacco from her tongue with delicate fingers. Exhaled. "Of course, my life would have been immeasurably better if I'd never had her, either."

Flannery didn't move or breathe. She had never heard this before. Any of it: Anne's French mother, their animosity.

"She used to pinch me, and slap me," Anne said. Half the cigarette had already disappeared. No one weak, Flannery thought, could smoke like that. "When she was annoyed with me. She'd slap my cheek—to wipe the smirk off it, she said." Anne stubbed the cigarette out vehemently. "I preferred smirking to crying. It bothered her more."

Flannery was cautious, still. But she did ask—she had to—

"How could anyone ever hurt that face?" She fit her palm around Anne's smooth cheek, stroked the loved line of her lips. "That beautiful face. How could anyone?"

For a second Anne's eyes were a different shade, the hurricane green Flannery had seen once or twice before. She pulled away from Flannery's hand, an uncharacteristically abrupt movement.

"You know what people are like," she said, in a voice graveled by old battles. She looked away, her face untouchable. "They're cruel, and they will do anything."

"You never did answer my question."

Another day, another diner. Anne, gourmet Anne, knew everything anyone could about the city's eating establishments. Greek, with infinite menus; Italian, steam-filled and carved-tabled; and American, all eggs and hash browns, like the Yankee Doodle.

"What question?"

"About your name. Come on. *Flannery.* How did that happen?"

"I did tell you: it was my mother." She crunched her toasted muffin, eyeing Anne's bacon. Flannery had recently decided to stop eating red meat for a mangle of reasons that had to do with politics and preference. Anne was skeptical, and tauntingly savored her carnivorous selections. "All right. It was my mother who named me, but I think the choice had something to do with my father."

"He was an O'Connor fan? Intrigued by the Southern grotesque? Struck by the way violence and redemption feature in her work?"

"Mmmhmm." It was easiest, mouth full, to agree.

"No." Anne, finished, pulled out a cigarette. She never bothered to wait till Flannery had finished eating. "You're not telling me everything here. You're holding back. What about your father? How does he fit in?"

"I don't know. I never knew him."

Anne put her cigarette down, unlit. "You didn't? Why— What happened to him?"

"I'm not sure. My mother wouldn't tell me. She always said that he was a good man, but that she lost him. Just—lost him. She wouldn't elaborate. Wouldn't say how."

Anne raised an eyebrow. "Maybe he was hard to find."

Flannery nodded, muffin-filled. "Well. Right. I know."

"Jesus." Anne lit up now. "No wonder you want to be a writer. How can you not, with all that behind you? You practically are a novel already."

Flannery shrugged modestly, as if her mysterious life were her own invention.

"So." Sped by the cigarette, Anne's mind moved rapidly. Finally! The biography interest. What had taken her so long? "What about your mother? She ever hook up with someone else?"

"Nope. It's just been the two of us." Flannery chewed. "For better or worse. Richer or poorer."

"And what does she do for a living? For richer or poorer?"

"Poorer, pretty often. She's an English teacher."

"Oh great. Like me!" Anne rolled her eyes. "So that's why you were attracted to me. I'm your *mother*. Of course. It all makes sense now."

"Well, you didn't think it was for your looks, did you?" Flannery brushed Anne's cheek with a buttery thumb—cautiously, so the other diners might not object or notice. "It was always going to be about your mind. Knowing you've read all those sexy volumes of literature stacked all over the place."

"I know." Anne sighed. A martyr. Pretty enough to die for. "I may as well accept it. You've only ever loved me for my shelves of books."

It was true, though. She did worship silently at Anne's bookshelves. She felt simultaneously a deep peace and a great excitement around Anne's apartment's white-painted shelves: the peace of knowing she was in the room that contained everything she'd ever need—Anne; food; a library—and the excitement of seeing how much was ahead of her to take in, comprehend, and ingest. Sometimes Flannery felt that excitement as a pulse in her fingers, a sharp sting in her eyes. She hadn't read *anything* yet. She had no idea of what everyone had already worked out about the world and love, and transcribed onto their pages. High school had given her thrills, certainly—Dostoevsky's ice-black moralism and Poe's ornate terrors, Shakespeare's many-splendored souls eloquizing fantastically. But Flannery's desire for more and better company was what had decided her on this forbidding institution, made her willing to brave the arduous trek out here. *Teach me*, she had quietly instructed, since the day she had arrived. *Get me started*.

Anne had recently, a significant trust, given Flannery keys to her apartment, and some afternoons Flannery came over to study. The place and its volumes seemed to protect her, like an amulet, from the small trivia of class-taking, the biting anxieties of deadlines. Papers due; tests to be taken; sentences in used paperbacks to be underlined; oral presentations to be coughed and blushed over. She could do all that. Flannery had a fast mind and she could argue well and she was fit, athletic, in her intelligence. If you gave her tricks to master, she could, obedient creature, perform them.

Anne's bookshelves seemed to have nothing to do with classes and textbooks; they stood above and outside that regimen, far from the minds that created divisions among kinds of knowledge, and placed them in categories for undergraduates (Arts, Language, Science) like the major food groups. Anne's books had no patience with the dumb, piecemeal task of making yourself smart; they promised something more ethereal, closer to wisdom.

Flannery especially noticed the shelves that spoke of Anne's work—Cather and Kate Chopin and their different notions of women's narratives. Those were the volumes (*My Ántonia*, *O Pioneers!*, *The Awakening*) visibly thumbed through, dozens of times, by Anne's watchful hands; their pages had been discovered and remembered by her adventurous green eyes. Through them Anne's supple mind had traveled, darting and acquisitive. Flannery looked over and loved them, those titles especially, and they filled her with envy: though whether of Anne for her knowledge or of the books themselves for the attention she lavished on them, Flannery couldn't have said.

Anne taught her how to eat.

Not that Flannery hadn't eaten before she knew Anne. She had. In the days prior to the soulless shovels of salad and pasta from the student dining halls, back where Flannery came from, she had even eaten well. She had a Californian's taste for greenery and whole grains, brown chunky baked goods; but she also had an eye for fruit, for the strange gifts from trees.

She knew things. She knew how to peel a pomegranate, unfolding the tart hidden pleasures of its intricately married seeds. She knew how loquats, with their buttery orange flesh and smooth, honed pits, were a better, rarer treat than the West's ubiquitous apricots. With protected hands she could pick a prickly pear off a cactus and later tease out from its dinosaur skin a pale pink heart that held the sweet perfume of dry summer.

"I could show you those things, if we were there." Flannery wanted Anne to understand that she had knowledge, too: there were secrets she could yield, too. "Here I can't show you anything."

In the meantime, bound as they were to the East, Anne taught Flannery how to eat.

She taught her the wisdom of ingredients, the principle of the simple best. It was the opposite strategy to the one Flannery had grown used to at the university, whose feeding principle was of quantity over quality: it may be bad, but there's a lot of it. A mess of items thrown together in a soup or stew, covered over with cheese or pastry to disguise any mistakes. Melt mozzarella over virtually anything, and a twenty-year-old will eat it.

Anne's kitchen was so sparsely outfitted it made Flannery nervous. How could any substantial food come out of here? (It was true, as Anne had once joked, that Flannery's bones were still growing.) But then she saw Anne's bottle of olive oil and was transfixed. She had never seen such a resonant, epic green before—not since the last time she'd looked into Anne's eyes.

With that oil and a tidy counterful of bread and vegetables, Anne made what seemed to Flannery to be the first genuine meal she'd ever eaten. Grilled eggplant, studded with roasted garlic, scattered with kosher salt and olive oil; crostini with a tomato and basil salsa, also grilled; and a risotto, something Flannery had never heard of, rich with some mushroom that had nothing to do with the gray rubbery disks she ate mostly on pizzas. A mushroom that spoke Italian, certainly. That spoke of other worlds. As did the wine they drank, a red whose name and provenance Anne explained carefully to Flannery, who instantly forgot it.

Finished, they were pungent and sated. Memories of garlic, wine, mushroom, salt, warmed their mouths.

It was Anne who hesitated a little, wondering . . .

And it was Flannery who insisted, promising that their kisses, as proved true, would be all the tastier.

"Do you remember seeing me at that diner—the Yankee Doodle? That morning?"

Lovers' languid indulgences: the sugared reconstruction of the narrative of their love. "And then you—" "And then I—" It's a fun game, for the two who can exclusively play it.

"You ordered a jelly omelette," said Anne. "How could I forget it?"

"And your first thought was 'Who is this intriguing, daring woman coming in and finding such a unique item on the menu?'"

"My first thought was 'Who's come in here at this hour with a kid?' But I looked around and there was no kid. And then—all in a flash—I realized *you* were the kid."

"And you immediately developed this Pygmalion fixation in which you thought, 'I shall take this unformed girl under my wing and teach her not to order jelly omelettes. I shall educate her.'"

"I looked over at the placer of this order and I thought, 'Hmm. She's cute. Why is she staring at me?'"

"Well," said Flannery—mostly fake-sulkily, but part of her pout was real—"I was busy falling in love at first sight. So I had to stare. That's what you do when you're falling in love at first sight. You go into soft focus, and romantic music starts playing in the background."

"Ah, so that's what that music was."

"But, no. See, you didn't hear the music. You were not experiencing love at first sight. You were concentrating too hard on your damn book." Flannery tapped Anne lightly on the cheek. Playful—a love slap. "What book was it, anyway? I've always wanted to ask you. I assumed it had to be something significant, like the book with all the answers to the world, or the *Kama Sutra*, or something."

"It was probably Bradley's book. His first class was later that morning and I was not especially prepared."

"Aha! So you do remember it. It was a significant encounter."

"Of course it was. This cute chick was watching me like a hawk as I drank my coffee. I was always going to notice that."

"Love at first sight. That's what I was going through."

"Lust at first sight. That's what I was going through."

Flannery sighed. "You know what?" she said. "That's good enough for me."

Sometimes, in the cooler periods, when they gave their physical love a brief vacation and settled into conversation, Flannery did not feel younger than Anne. She felt older, even, and an anchor, definitely: she could tell that was what Anne needed—someone to hold her down, to give her ballast. Anne was not floaty or dreamy—that was Flannery, who could spend an hour staring at the windowed sky when she should be reading and, when asked what she was up to, had to answer, "Nothing. Thinking." But Anne was fundamentally unattached. It worried Flannery; not for herself, but for Anne. It made her want to hold Anne close, and also just to stay still for her, so that she'd know she could come back to Flannery and find that Flannery was still there.

Anne wouldn't tell her. She wouldn't tell her what it was. "I get depressed sometimes," she'd said. "That's all." "So do I," Flannery said. "Once, when—" "Yes, well, I guess everyone does." Flannery agreed. —Yes, of course other people, too, but that wasn't what mattered to her. What mattered to her was Anne. If she waited, and was quiet, Anne might finally speak.

Anne did speak. She told Flannery a few distant stories of an earlier life—"when I was someone else," back in Michigan. Stories of her ferocious grandfather, a failed composer, and how he'd demanded from her years of arduous pretense that she might one

158

day be a pianist. Her sister Patricia's assigned vocation was dance—years of ballet lessons. Neither had stuck with it; the instant the grandfather died, they'd abandoned all trappings of these phantom careers. "Do you still play?" Flannery had asked when she heard the story.

"Almost never."

"Hmmm."

"'Hmmm'—what?" Anne demanded. Spiky. "What?"

"Nothing, sweetheart. Just that you will again sometime, I bet. Somewhere else. Sometime—else." Flannery said it with a sureness that made Anne seem young, and quiet, and a little rebellious.

"Yes. That's what—" she started. Then stopped.

That long dash, that hesitation: it came up at other times, too. Flannery heard it, but did not draw attention to it. She was aware of this space that Anne carefully sidestepped, and the more Anne didn't say, the more sense Flannery had of the contours of her silence: the shape of what she kept unsaid. Flannery felt old, knowing that this unspoken place was in Anne and that it remained untouched by Flannery. She knew she'd never get at it. Either because no one ever would; or because someone else already had.

"I love you," Anne told her somberly. "You're such a good soul, Flannery. I'm lucky. I'm lucky . . ?" She couldn't finish the sentence.

Flannery loved to hear it, but she felt old knowing more than Anne knew.

"I could lie in your arms for years," Anne said to Flannery. But, privately, Flannery suspected she wouldn't.

It was when Anne spoke of her travels that Flannery felt young. Anne had already had so many adventures, and by comparison Flannery had had none. (A week in England with her mother when she was a sulky teenager and a drugged weekend in Santa Cruz with other high-school renegades hardly counted.) Anne had driven across the country through Louisiana and Texas and Arizona, all places that were mere resonant names for Flannery, not genuine geographies. Anne had been to Berlin for the film festival on a junket with a journalist friend, and from there had taken a train to Warsaw, "just to see it." (Her father's family was Polish—another provocative fact she left unadorned by detail or explanation.) She had bussed around Mexico in the dust, seeing ancient buildings and tiny villages with someone she knew who was doing fieldwork there. The companions on these enter-prises were shadowy figures, and Flannery could not tell from Anne's few clues whether they were friends or "friends." She did not ask.

The country Anne had visited most, though, and the one Flannery most wanted, was France. Paris, mostly. (Anne's mother's city, Flannery noted, but did not say.) Anne had spent so much time in Paris that she forgot what people who haven't might not know about it: the meaning of "Left Bank" and "Right Bank," for instance, or what "in the Fifth" might refer to. "That's an empty signifier," Flannery might have said in parody of their former shared Criticism, but she didn't want to admit her ignorance. She was jealous. The other places Anne had been to, Flannery was satisfied to give her; Anne deserved them, and Flannery felt generous about them. (It was the same as with a love's past lovers: there are the ones you indulge and can hear tales of, and the ones who get under the skin, for some reason, that you might have to shoot on meeting.) Flannery could get to those places herself, later. There was, as Anne sometimes gently—was it condescendingly?—reminded her, plenty of time.

But Paris she wanted. Flannery wanted it now. She couldn't wait. Couldn't they go together? Couldn't they? Over spring break?

"Not in the spring," Anne said. "Not then. In the summer, maybe."

Paris in the summer? Flannery's blood and imagination quickened. She was already there. She threw all caution—the caution that might have asked how likely this plan might really be, what with the high cost and complex logistics—into the wintered air and prepared, in her fanciful, romantic head, for summer in Paris. With her Anne.

"You know what I'd like?"

It took Anne's voice some time to penetrate Flannery's busy excitement. Finally: "What?"

"To go somewhere I've never been before, with you. Somewhere crazy and exotic—somewhere full of people not like anyone here."

"Like where?" Flannery liked the sound of this.

"Like Florida."

"*Florida?*" The word was almost offensive to Flannery's western ears. Florida! Wasn't it just a cheap, plastic version of the real thing—California?

"Florida," Anne repeated. "In the spring."

That settled it. That's where they'd go.

Anne was not, on the pretty face of it, a kind person. She was too edged for that. Unlike Flannery, whose smile warmed and reassured people, letting them know she was sweetly harmless—an impression, Anne remarked, that was altogether misleading—Anne's countenance kept people on their guard. Her intense attractiveness was forbidding, even as it compelled and beckoned. People simultaneously wanted and feared her. Flannery saw it all the time, and remembered it from her earlier quaking self.

Flannery now had privileged information, of course, about the alluring, elusive scholar. Flannery knew her secrets and frailties, at least a few of them. She knew where the scars were, and how Anne slept (on her side, an arm usually flung up, protectively), and what she looked like when she was less than put together. (Ravishing, still. Always ravishing.) She knew the scent Anne wore and her favorite foods (she was partial to gingerbread) and the color of her underclothes (white; you wouldn't think so). And Flannery knew something else, too, a truth she held close to her like a jewel, where others couldn't see it or try to take it from her. It was, per-haps—this truth—the heart of what Flannery had discovered about her.

Anne was kind.

162

She covered Flannery in kindnesses all over, as if they were kisses. For long, slow minutes she'd knead Flannery's overstudied shoulders. She made a warming morning bowl of oatmeal with toasted walnuts and plump raisins—good for the brain, she claimed. She'd find books from friends she knew Flannery had searched for fruitlessly at the library, or track down a troublesome reference that had gnawed at Flannery's mind for days. When Flannery spoke of her cold feet, Anne bought her beautifully soft wool socks, and when Flannery mentioned her hands were chapped by winter air, Anne produced a soothing aromatic lotion. She did not ask for an audience for these kindnesses; she just generously performed them.

And that wasn't everything. Best of all, Anne read to her.

First things first: when these treats began, it was Marilyn Hacker's poems Flannery had to hear Anne read. Soon after their meeting in New York, back in the primeval dawn of this epic passion, Flannery had questioned her former TA about the gift.

"What were you doing?" As they lay sprawled, she pulled on Anne's hair, half-playfully, half-painfully. "Giving me that book?"

"It's obvious what I was doing." Anne let her head be tugged in punishment. "I was corrupting a minor. Ow! Okay. That's enough."

"I should sue you for sexual harassment."

"I hope you won't."

"And then you'd be convicted, of course, because I'd break down in court, thus earning the pitying sympathy of everyone on the jury—"

"'*J'accuse!*' you'd say, pointing at me, in a cute French accent that would only help your case—"

"And they'd think how sad it was that this sweet, innocent girl—"

"With a filthy imagination, who was actually a nymphomaniac—"

"Yeah, but they'd never believe that. Anyway, stop interrupting, you're the defendant. —That this sweet, innocent girl, a westerner from a one-horse town, who didn't know anything from anything and actually had to be bought a pair of sunglasses to disguise her wide-eyed, fresh-faced virginity—"

Anne rolled her eyes.

"—was seduced! By this wily older woman. Who had in fact bought the sunglasses in a premeditated move, yes!, so that she could smuggle this minor up to the evil lair she had carefully prepared, where unbeknownst to an indifferent outside world, this young maiden was—how shall we put it delicately—"

"'Plucked' or 'deflowered' would be consistent with your rhetoric at this point."

"Exactly. Where she was *plucked*." Flannery finally stopped pulling Anne's hair and stroked it instead. "Plucked! Ladies and gentlemen of the jury, I rest my case."

She was flushed, triumphant with the victory of her oration. "I should be a lawyer," she said.

"You should be a writer." Anne tugged Flannery's fair hair in return. "That vivid fantasy life of yours. It was you who seduced me, missy, as I recall. And I've got a memory for such details."

"Hmmm. So you say." Flannery flopped back, head on pillow. She grimaced, as if in sorrowful regret. "But it's your word against mine, sweetheart. Whose do you think they're more likely to trust?"

Anne's punishment, the court decided, meeting in closed session in Anne's bedroom, was to perform one hundred hours of community service. The community in question was Flannery. The service—"Don't be obscene!" scolded Flannery, when Anne made a lewd expression—was to read.

"Read? I do that anyway. I'll already have completed my sentence, retroactively. I'm out! I'm free."

"Not reading to yourself. Reading out *loud*. To the *community*. That's the service."

It was one Anne was happy to provide. In the same way that she collected admiring glances from the world, a knowing diva gathering deserved bouquets, so also did Anne gather compliments for her voice. She anticipated the liquid pleasure brought on by the sound of it. She knew it melted people. Flannery had noticed, the single morning she'd sat as a student in Anne's class (when, in furious mortification, she had pretended not to be listening), the strategic dip to a lower, slower register, in a moment when Anne needed to capture her students' undivided attention. The sultry tone—redolent of a steamy bathhouse, hot with pungent flowers and oiled muscles and slippery ministrations—made slaves of its listeners. She captivated them. She roped them in.

And it was Flannery's kingliest privilege to have this voice all to herself. *Mine!* she sometimes murmured in astonishment. *She's mine.*

These deeply pleasurable command reading performances gradually shifted, figuratively. From Anne the fallen prisoner doing penance, to Anne the subject performing her duty to liege nobility; and from there, in an apt turning of the tables, to Anne the star actress rehearsing her lines for her besotted director. By then, as March approached, suggesting the possibility of spring, Anne had traveled through Sexton and Bishop on to Dylan Thomas and Eliot, and was taking a vacation in prose narrative by request. Cortázar and Kincaid, for old times' sake, and Grace Paley, because she was irresistible, and, inevitably, O'Connor: Flannery had to know how that great writer sounded in the voice of the woman who had discovered her namesake.

Once, as a surprise, Anne announced she wanted to read to Flannery from a new author, a young talent who she was sure would one day make a mark on the world. Flannery was too distracted to see it coming. When she heard that honeyed voice pronounce the familiar lines

> *I'd like to pay your palms*
> *the same favor that you pay these pages*

she howled in agony and pelted her reader with a hail of pillows. The actress, deterred by the assault, had to stop, but not before telling her audience, laughingly,

"You'll see! One day they'll all be reading her. One day"—she dodged the pillows and ran from the room, warning on her way out—"you'll look back on this performance as a moment in history!"

"So what's this one?" Anne challenged.

Flannery kissed Anne, searchingly, on lips that beckoned with a decorative, delicate purplish red. Not so bright as to be teenager-ish and gaudy, but not so dark as to belong to a rich woman's wife or a model.

"What's your guess?" Anne asked. "What does the color look like to you?" They were playing a makeup game, an attempt to educate Flannery in the feminine arts, in which she was mournfully untrained.

"Mmmm." Flannery kissed her again, as if she could determine the answer by feel. "Raspberry Sherbet?"

"God, no!" Anne pulled away in distaste. "That's so trashy. My lipsticks never have names like that."

"Okay. Wait. Something rosy? Rose Garden? Rose Treat?"

"Better. That's close. Rose *Beautiful*."

"Beautiful. Well. That goes without saying. Are they all called beautiful?"

Anne disappeared into the bathroom and came back wearing a subtle plum. The color for a night at the theater or a chic Japanese restaurant.

"Dusk Delight? Luscious Lavender? No—Lavender Menace."

"You'll never get a job doing this. Even with all your verbal skills. *Mauve Amour.*"

"I'd have a better chance if I'd ever worn the stuff myself. You have to bear in mind, I'm a novice—I mean, I don't even know which aisle of the drugstore it is."

"I know. It's sweet: you're a cosmetics virgin. Another way I'm deflowering you. Here"—Anne disappeared into the bathroom again—"I'm going to find some to put on you."

"That's a little perverse, isn't it?" Flannery called. "You know who would be into that? Murphy. Our old friend Murphy, in New York. I think Murphy would enjoy this."

Anne came back. She insisted that Flannery close her eyes. Flannery felt the breath of her lover, and her concentration. At the smooth, cool, not quite sensual marking of her lips she immediately started laughing.

"Stop! Or it will smear."

"I can't help it, it tickles."

Flannery kept her mouth as still as she could while her makeup artist finished, then got up to look at herself in the mirror. Her face looked completely different. Unrecognizable. She looked a decade older, for one thing; no longer a child. This was someone who had had experiences in the world, and who knew where she was going.

"Go ahead!" Anne laughed. "Guess the color."

"My God. What have you done to me?" Her mouth was a vivid, femme-fatale red.

"Guess. One word. An adjective. Sounds like—"

" 'Whorish'? 'Obscene'?"

"*Outrageous.*"

"Outrageous. They're right." Still, Flannery couldn't quite leave her reflection alone. It fascinated her. "Your turn," she said vaguely, waving Anne back to the bathroom. What would someone be like, who wore this color lipstick?

"Last one," Anne said. "My lips are worn out."

She went into the bathroom and emerged a few minutes later, her own lips a dark red—darker than Flannery's, but as much of a bold statement. The look was so striking it diverted Flannery finally from the distraction of her new personality.

"Whoo, baby!" Flannery catcalled.

"No. It's not called Whoo, Baby."

"Well, it should be. We'd make a good pair."

"This one is something more literary. I thought you might like that."

"Literary? What—Red Badge of Courage?"

"No."

"The Fire Next Time?"

"Oh! Great guess. Close. Frenchier."

"Oooh-la-la?"

"Bad guess. Le Rouge et le Noir."

"God, that *is* literary. You must be a classy broad."

"I am. And my makeup is classy, too."

"Of course it is," said Outrageous, coming over to meet her. "It's very classy. I like that in a broad." She pulled Le Rouge et le Noir down with her onto the bed. "Now come here, *chérie*, where I can kiss it all off you."

They played each other their signature tunes. Each had favorites to warble to the other—precious lyrics from songwriters' ballads or classic rock numbers, catchy riffs from current hits that prompted private dancing, or string quartets to bring on more interior reflection. They played them in and out of love and work together, combining and refining their musical libraries until it was hard to remember what they'd listened to before they knew each other.

From Anne, Flannery learned jazz.

It was not an idiom she had picked up before: it existed, a whole country, just outside the places she could find her way around in. Flannery was sure that all the best and smartest people liked jazz—the guitarist she'd once had a crush on; her close high-school friend, a proud aficionado; Nick—so she tried now to adjust her own ear to its rhythms and suggestions.

Anne played her Monk. She played Flannery many people, brass players or pianists, new ensembles or old masters, but it was Monk that took. When Flannery heard *Blue Monk*, she understood something of the form's wit and artistry. She began to get it. It helped that she could listen to him while watching what he did to Anne. When Monk was on—when Anne was cooking, often, because she cooked best to song, and sang best while cooking—

Anne was freed and transformed. He loosened her and provoked her. He met her spirit somewhere Flannery had never encountered it, and they spoke to each other there, privately, trading jokes and concerns. It was hard, in a strange way, not to be jealous.

One night, late February and sleeting, not long before spring break, Flannery waited outside the door to Anne's apartment before going in. She held her precious set of keys, to her haven here, in her hand.

She heard Anne's voice inside, and music and laughter. It sounded like a party. Flannery wondered if she'd forgotten some social event. Was Anne having friends over to dinner? Was it a night Flannery was meant to stay back in the dorm?

She knocked lightly and a hectic voice called out, "Come in!" so she did, braced for company and rowdiness.

Inside was Anne at the stove, cheeks pinkish with wine or dancing. The lights were soft. The music was loud. Anne did not stop what she was doing, so Flannery watched her a moment. She was moving—not dancing, exactly; something more like her body's rising to meet the cadences. Swimming, or flying. It was Monk. Anne's eyes were closed as she listened, swayed, lost herself to the sensation. Flannery could see the fact all over Anne, in her dreamy hands and smiling mouth, in the ease and desire of her empty arms: she was in love with Thelonius Monk. And—this was harder to know, but it nipped at Flannery suddenly, a bitter suspicion—he reminded her of someone else she loved, too.

It wasn't Flannery.

PART THREE

In Florida, it went wrong. Something started to fade. Flannery did not fade, but Anne did.

Florida had always felt wrong to Flannery, even before it assaulted her skin and scared her witless. The place was Anne's determined choice, based, as Flannery slowly realized, on a downward mobility of taste: she sought the kitsch and tacky, the anti-university, while Flannery was on the escalator going the other way—up, hopefully, toward Baudelaire and risotto and airplane travel to any place that was not America.

For Flannery this state had always seemed gaudy and improbable, a place where Walt Disney had felt hyperbolic enough to build a World rather than just a Land. (Flannery had vacationed in his Land when she was a child, with her mother, and knew its rides, songs, and foods as the best and original.) Anne said she wanted to see the Everglades, a tempting word but one that brought to Flannery's mind images of shady, well-tended golf courses or hushed, tidy cemeteries. She had no idea what the "Everglades" were. To Flannery Florida was orange juice, launchpads for space trips, and old people, and whatever might be meant by the slippery name *Miami*.

Miami was not even on their menu. Anne planned the locations and days, the entire itinerary. Passive Flannery followed, dreaming wistfully of Paris. Paris was where they should have been. It had the language, the taste for their passion. In Paris they could have savored foods Flannery found vile in English, and Anne would have taught Flannery a few French phrases (beyond *chérie* and *amour*), delighting over the sound of them on Flannery's lips. The city's light would have silvered them. One woman would have bought the other one *des fleurs*. They would have gone to an evening concert in a cathedral, where the orchestra's harmonies reaching to the domed stone ceiling would have made Flannery think she had heard the music of the spheres. And Flannery would have written something beautiful, afterward; she was sure of it. She would have made that overloved and overwritten-about city hers, and theirs.

Flannery remained certain, even once she became older and smarter and pessimism ran through her veins, that their story would have gone differently if they had traveled to Paris instead.

They took the train down. Anne's idea: it was cheaper than flying, though it would take them over twenty-four hours to get there. Initially Flannery was itchy and squeamish at the idea of those long Amtrak hours, but as Anne pointed out, it gave them "more bang for their buck," more states per dollar. "Think of all the places we'll go through on our way to Tampa," Anne said to her, but Flannery could not think of them beforehand; her geography was not good enough. If Anne had told her the journey would route them through Louisiana and Kentucky, Flannery would have believed her.

It did not, but it did take them through Washington, D.C., where they had several hours' layover, enough time to leave the station and take in the highly organized grandeur of the nation's segregated capital. Flannery knew of her own state's racial iniquities—the more so since enrolling in a self-improving course on the Ethnic and Labor History of the West—but she had never seen the divide made so visible. It gave her a shocked inkling of how the country's race disease might look south of Mason-Dixon. (Not that she could have located the Mason-Dixon line, either.) Back on the train south, Flannery listened to a jovial black conductor speaking in two distinct registers: polite and joky to white passengers, warmly intimate with African Americans. These were new tones to her.

One of Flannery's favorite discoveries occurred in the dining car. Grits, a mythic-sounding food, turned out to be a gummy hot cereal served in a Styrofoam dish. Anne frequently fled their seats to smoke in the card-playing car, as she called it, but the thick choke of air there was too much for Flannery. She'd rather sit at her foldable table, flipping back and forth anxiously between the unlikelihood of free will (Mortal Questions: Intro to Philosophy) and the early slaughter of the natives by all the gold-rush forty-niners she had been schooled to revere.

Out the humidity-streaked window, damp new lands unspooled, frame by frame. The women moved through the Carolinas in the middle of the night and woke to a sun-kissed Georgia. It was warm and beautiful and foreign, busy with unknown demons, and Flannery felt uneasiness, like an insect, crawling all over her.

The state's first act was to sear Flannery's flesh. They had scarcely arrived, had had time only to stumble, dazed, from the train and out into the morning light of Tampa, collect their rental car, and hit the road for as long as it took to get to a decent beach. Twenty minutes. It was too early to find what they really needed—a bed and a shower—so they took what was available in the interim. Water. Sand. *Sun.*

Flannery had never been a sun-worshipper, or a beach babe. She had the body but not the mind for it. Crucially, she had the wrong skin. It was the least western thing about her: her pallor, which gave her a shy unwillingness to throw her body into the elements. Clothed, she could go anywhere—rock, creek, forest, hillside—but unclothed, she quailed. Fear pricked her skin with rash memories and burn worry.

After a brief beachside amble, taking in soft drinks and T-shirts and the buying of a pumpkin-orange beach ball to play with (ironically, of course), the girls sunbathed together. Flannery's long shape covering a vast blue towel with a shark pictured on it, Anne on a paper-thin spread that read THE SUNSHINE STATE, like the license plates.

Anne, in spite of her own redheaded coloring, lay down with a sigh of satisfaction that seemed almost orgasmic. She threw open her arms and heart to the heat. "Thank God," she kept saying. "We're out of that fucking train. Out of that fucking winter. Out of that fucking *university*." Already "university" had a strange sound in her mouth, as if she were eating a pickle: the word puckered and crinkled, and Flannery did not understand the source of her vinegar. There was a hovering in Anne's thought that Flannery had not identified, a flicker that hazeled Anne's green eyes and diverted her fonder attentions. Why "fucking" university? What was so wrong about the place that had, after all, brought them together? It might be full of pompous rigidities, as they both agreed, and it might be a self-important place, grandiose, intolerant of outsiders; but it was theirs, too. Their own private school for scandal, as the joke had gone.

"New Mexico," Anne said into the stern light overhead, "would not have those fucking winters." New Mexico had begun to make awkward appearances in the sentences between them, a guest Flannery had not welcomed.

"They get snow in New Mexico, too," she said. "In the winter."

"Really?" Anne turned skeptical blue shades in her direction, as if Flannery were a precocious student. "How do you know that?"

Flannery kicked her, drawing a loud "Ouch!" from THE SUN-SHINE STATE. They were both restless from the airless train hours and needed the wrestling match they would fall into later at their terrible motel. "Because I'm not a complete idiot," Flannery told her. "I do know some things." She lay back on the sand, placing a hand over her irritated eyes.

"Oh yes. So you keep saying." Anne's voice was smug and lazy in the moist heat, lulling Flannery into a near-doze. "So you keep telling me." Anne sat up to cover her limbs and chest in a thin layer of sunblock; then neglected to pass the tube, after, to her forgetful, fair-skinned lover.

It was after the seafood, wrestling, and squab-bling that the pain set in.

Travel can be so full of quibbles and snivelings, if two people don't know or can't agree on where they are going. Flannery had not wanted this trip, anyway. The clarity of the fact emerged in the far-too-bright sunlight, which was, as she had always suspected, more garish and show-offy than the subtler sunlight she had grown up with; nor was it dignified by blue foothills or grander, more distant mountains. Here there was no land to take hold of beyond the relentless beach and its picture-perfect blue ocean, and no pair of sunglasses could fend off all the color and visual noise that besieged her. When Anne suggested in the afternoon that they drive south down the coast, to close in on the Everglades, Flannery balked.

"Not more time cooped up," she said, in a voice perilously close to a whine. The poison snaking around her interior had not yet burst out into open crimson—Flannery had no idea how much damage she had done to herself—but sun-sickness soured her and made her an unruly child.

"What, you want to stay somewhere around here?" Anne waved a hand at beachfront hotels shaded in pastels and cocktails. "Too expensive, babe. We're not this class of traveler—not after

183

the car and the train tickets. Unless you're planning to lease out your nubile body to some rich old golfers—?"

Flannery was not prepared to get any kind of joke. "Not *here*," she sulked. "Some motel somewhere. I don't care where. Just not more time cooped up. I can't stand it."

No answer. Flannery felt Anne's coolness breeze over her, but in truth it was a relief after the enervating heat.

So they compromised, often the worst plan, and drove out of Tampa as far as Sarasota, where they found a motel off the highway. The town was the Home of the Ringling Museum of Art, a proud sign informed them, but by now such an idea could only depress them: they were past being able to enjoy the name's carnival associations. They found a deserted restaurant, where they ate bad fried shrimp and ran out of subjects to talk about, then returned to their cheap room nauseous and grouchy. Across a scratchy bedspread they chose not to love but to wrestle, a little too sincerely. Already Flannery felt sore—Anne crowed over her victory, and claimed that Flannery was faking her pain, out of bad sportsmanship—but it was when she tried showering and the pellets of water felt like acid rain on her protesting skin that Flannery realized something bad had happened to her. She called out in agony, to an answering silence from the room. Anne seemed unable to greet the news of Flannery's ailment with anything other than a bland "Oh, that's too bad."

Which led to Flannery's spending a long, wide-eyed night on the other side of the bed from her tossing, fast-asleep lover. The feverish pain allowed Flannery to indulge the sensation that her case was terminal and she would be waking up dead. Even the light sheets seemed like enemies to Flannery as she shivered in her terrible sunburn, feeling the Florida sun break back out of her lobster-red body in vicious, hot waves, and hallucinating a dry voice that told her, already, it was time to go home.

Flannery woke in the tart dawn light that filtered through the salt-faded curtains. A dim claustrophobia hung in the air like a storm cloud. Anne was sitting by the dresser. Dressed.

"Isn't it early, to be up and ready? Where are you going?" Flannery could not rub the sleep from her eyes: they hurt too much.

"I thought I might take a walk."

"Oh." She yawned. "God, this place reeks. It looks even worse in the daylight."

"It's a vile place. There are probably rats napping in the corner." Anne lit up.

"Hey, do you mind"—Flannery said, without thinking about it—"not doing that in here? If you're about to go out anyway—"

"Oh, *fine*." Anne stubbed the cigarette out violently in the tin ashtray stamped with the motel logo, THE BEACHCOMBER. She stood to go out.

"Sorry, it's just that—"

"Fine. I'm going."

"All I meant was," Flannery stumbled, "you've been smoking so much lately, and sometimes—"

"Oh, here we go." Anne's voice was caustic. "I should really cut down a little? I thought you thought my smoking was sexy. A great turn-on."

"I do. It's just—" Flannery was too hot to be able to think of the right way to put it.

"So sexy that you took it up, too, so you'd taste like me. That was so sweet." How bitter she sounded!

"I did, I did." A sting started at Flannery's eyes. Don't cry, for God's sake, she instructed herself. That would humiliate them both. Instead, she breathed for a moment, to the extent it was possible. "I did, until you told me I looked stupid doing it."

"Well." Anne shrugged, as if she were not to blame for the remark. "You did."

Then she grabbed her cigarettes and went out the cardboard-thin door. Leaving Flannery cool and burning, writhing in the discomfort of her blistering skin.

What was the matter?

What hand had come down to block the light between them, and what relation did it have to the words "University of New Mexico"? Anne was awaiting final word about the job there, and Flannery understood that the uncertainty gnawed at her. She had flown out to Albuquerque in late February to perform her "dance of the seven veils" for the full complement of hirers and would-be colleagues: guest-lecturing, meeting students and other faculty. (It had been a mournful four-day absence but one that allowed Flannery to catch up on Physics for Poets—her science credit—at last.) The signs from that outing were good. "They loved me; they ate me up" was Anne's optimistic view, borne out by a faculty member who called to tell Anne, off the record, that they wanted her for the job. The committee just had to move through its slow bureaucracy.

So that was all good news. Wasn't it? Not for Flannery, for whom Anne's distance next year in New Mexico was a heart wreck waiting to happen. But for *Anne* it was good news. So why was she so testy? "I'm sure you've got the job," Flannery had said to her in mid-Virginia on the train down, to which Anne had snapped, "You don't have any idea what you're talking about."

As Anne walked that morning, wherever she might be, the heat kept up its attack on Flannery inside, making her want to sink into the cool softness of a soak in cold lotion or soothe herself by bathing in aloe. She lay spread out flat, limbs flying across the motel bed, hoping the shadowed fetid air was taking from her, slowly, some of the trapped sun. She was thirsty all the time and drank often from a plastic cup of foul-tasting water.

Maybe, her burned brain reasoned, this was how it went between people: silences, sulks, mysteries. The down times, about which there were fewer poems and rock songs. It could not all be love in the afternoon and passion at night, gifts given, notes written, meals fed to each other. Poetry read out loud over sheets still damp from earlier wordless activities. Slow dances while cooking, lingering kisses to Monk. *It can't all be like that, Flannery.* There had to be the pulling of ugly faces and sudden mutual waves of distaste, annoyance passed back and forth, one to the other, like a hot potato.

Flannery hoped, painfully. She tossed in restless, guessing doubt. And somewhere under the scald and the referred anger (*Anne* was the one who had planned this damned trip to this ridiculous state; and by the way, why had she failed to give Flannery the sunblock?)—somewhere under there, Flannery sensed, ingenue though she was, that this tension might not be in the normal run of a long-lasting love.

Something was wrong.

They drove. It can be a cure-all: the eating of miles can satisfy a hunger other foods cannot.

Flannery drove first, to atone (for what?), or at least to bring the softer curves of tolerance back to Anne's sharp-lined face. They did not speak. Flannery tried the radio, but the fuzzy sound of outdated hits filled the car with even more tense static, and soon she spun the knob back. *Off*; silence. It was the better position for them just now.

After a couple of hours, Flannery admitted, in an embarrassed mutter, that the pain was unbearable and she would have to find lotion, so they broke off from the road at a sprawling shopping center. In a vast sell-all drugstore Flannery found three kinds of after-sun care while Anne stocked up on tapes, mostly of country-and-western compilations, which were to become the sound track of their uncomfortable journey. They went for a late breakfast at a Shoney's, a place Flannery translated to herself as the Denny's of the South—it had similar bright colors and that open, booth-easy layout. She and her mother used to make runs to Denny's for pancakes, and the place made her homesick for that loved person she had paid so little attention to lately. Her mother. How was she? Flannery ought to send her a postcard. "Guess what! I'm in Florida. A friend and I are driving around, having a great time . . ."

Wordless, the women ate their breakfast. Flannery gained solace from a stack of pancakes smothered in syrup and thoughts of her mother, while Anne dryly crunched her way through crisp bacon and toast. Finally Flannery excused herself from her uncompanionable companion and took her gels and creams to the bathroom, where, with a few minutes to herself, she broke down and cried. Her flesh made her wince and dehydration pounded her head, and she succumbed to an underslept panic that she had, for no obvious reason, become insufferable to her own adored girlfriend.

"Oh, *honey*." A waitress in a corn-yellow uniform and hair to match came out of one of the stalls and looked at Flannery in the fluorescent-lit mirror with a lipsticked frown of imagined pain. "That is a *bad* burn. Look at you, you poor little thing." The *you* was a long *ewe*, a drawn-out taffy sound, sweet with sympathy. Flannery wanted to embrace her for it with her flame-skinned arms.

"I forgot the sunblock," she sniffed, unafraid now, away from Anne, to sound like the dumb kid she was.

"People do it all the time. They just forget how strong that sun can be. Have you tried butter?"

Flannery shook her head. "I've got all these creams . . ."

The waitress shook her high head as she checked her hair in the mirror. "Don't use those, honey. Try butter. It sounds crazy, but it's very soothing. I swear by a little butter on a bad burn. And you be careful—stay out of the daylight, it will only make it hurt worse."

Flannery thanked her, cleared up her tears, and returned to the table feeling better. At least she had an ally now against the punishing sun. When Anne went to the register to pay the check, Flannery grabbed a fat handful of butter pats and put them into her bag. She planned to try the waitress's trick later on, when Anne wasn't watching. She would be bound to laugh.

But in all that followed, of course, Flannery forgot about the butter. So that another legacy of their blighted vacation was a series of books marked with translucent pages from the melting butter's calming, widespread salve.

From the fast unhappy car, Flannery saw silver. By the roadside. A still, mournful huddle of luminous fur. But large: person-sized, legend-sized, not the dimension of some poor dog or possum.

"Wait. Slow down. Do you see that?'

"What?" Anne kept driving. She slowed down, fractionally.

"Slow down! Wait. Did you—" Flannery craned her head back, chafing her chest against the seatbelt. "Ouch—*shit*. Did you see that?"

"What?'

Eyeless and soulless as far as Flannery could tell, behind the sunglasses. Mouth unmoved. Skin smooth, soft, lightly tan: flawless.

"Are you even in there anymore?" Flannery wondered, under her breath.

That got Anne's attention.

"What did you say?" The car slowed, but it was too late now. Her voice was dangerous. "What did you say to me?"

"Why didn't you stop?"

"For what? You didn't say what you saw."

"Because it was so sad and awful." Flannery, as a kind of rebellious statement, took her own sunglasses off. She squinted sorely into the unforgiving sky that waited at the end of this straight, Everglade-edged road.

"Well, what was it?" Anne sped back up.

"Never mind."

"Don't be childish, Flannery. What was it?"

She sighed. "A panther."

"What do you mean, a panther?"

"A silver panther. Dead. By the side of the road."

"No." But she was impressed; almost willing to believe. "I don't think that's possible. What did it look like?"

"It was terrible. I don't want to talk about it." Flannery knew perfectly well that such withholding really did seem childish. But she was not keeping quiet out of a pouting, kidlike retribution. That dead silver body had filled her stomach with a genuine ill ease and a hollow feeling of loss. You did not have to be Florida-tolerant, as Flannery still wasn't, to figure out that such panthers were rare, that their numbers could not afford to be lowered by impatient, speeding vacationers. It was all wrong. But this was, in the silent car, unsayable. Newly shy Flannery was not tempted to explain the shape of this grief to the unmovable driver beside her.

The Everglades were unfathomable, eerie and steam-jungled, a natural riot unlike any western wildness Flannery had trekked through. In the Everglades she calmed down. They both did. It shut them both up, dwarfing their trivial disagreements as the planet's magnitudes sometimes can. (Who were they to bicker when all this was going on around them?) The Everglades made Flannery stop talking about Florida's ugly tackiness long enough to realize the place contained worlds inventive beyond Disney and shows more daring than Ringling's greatest on earth: that this state's heart was much darker and more interesting than she had, in her ignorance, believed. This was someplace worth getting to. It was worth the sunburn and brain fever; it might even be worth the inevitable heartache. Not that the heartache had arrived yet. It was to come.

And the Everglades were the first substance successful in soothing Flannery's sore skin. The sultry moisture of the place embraced her in something uncannily like comfort. *Uncanny*, because Flannery felt sure there were creeping disasters hidden in the swampy woods—not only in the shape of the hardly credible gators.

They walked. Starting at a tourist information panel near the parking lot, which listed the creatures and greeneries that raced through the strange Everglades. It was near a creek where a mother alligator and her brood dog-paddled photogenically. The women were helpless to find the baby alligators anything but adorable. Their not quite rough hides glistened a wet, dangerous jade that Flannery recognized as the color of those eyes that did not, just now, seem able to meet hers. But the whole landscape was rich in that familiar Anne color, the color of jealousy: all their surroundings seemed to be one insidious green or another. Sparse woods, but not as Flannery knew woods. Hers were pine and redwood and dry, or if not dry, then full of the thick yeast of fog. These woods were stooped, saturated with an unfamiliar atmosphere, and oozing with life forms unlike anywhere else. Flannery, generally unsuperstitious, felt ghosts hover over her flesh, and even Anne—rational, hard-minded Anne—looked spooked. She took off her sunglasses, at last, and let the mysteries in. And for that one act, that brief baring of soul, Flannery again loved her and loved Florida and felt, for the first time since the burn, the prickly inklings of desire.

On a dark path, they embraced. Flannery wore cheap turquoise shorts she had bought as a joke back in Sarasota and a long tank top that yawned lazily over her lean frame. Anne, who always knew better, was in one of her crisp white T's and denim shorts that would have looked boyish or butch on a less feminine body. Flannery loved her that way: tough girl, a bit of swagger on the outside, and all girl, all softness, just underneath. That was Anne all over.

"Come here." Flannery breathed in an air that hummed with multiplications of flora and fauna.

"I *am* here." Anne slid her tongue into Flannery's ear to prove it, and sidled up even closer. What a relief, to have shed their recent dislike and suspicion. Here they were: back. Relieved Flannery containing her Anne; relaxed Anne editing her Flannery. She put a light finger on Flannery's lips. "Does it hurt a lot?" It was the first time she had acknowledged the affliction as anything other than Flannery's irritating fault.

"It hurts," Flannery said in a hushed voice. "But it hurts so *good*."

"Ooh, baby," Anne hushed back. "As Murphy might say." She urged her smile onto Flannery's.

"Mmm" was all Flannery could manage to that, before she let herself swallow and give way. Kissing, in any case, was only good, as Flannery's mouth was unscarred by the sun. And kissing remained an index of their proximity: the two women could not kiss unless their spirits were close, and when there was distance between them their mouths avoided each other. They had kissed maybe once or twice since the morning they'd first boarded the train. There was always the excuse—as there is, between two women tempting fate with this kind of adventure—that, unless they were deeply barricaded and private, people might see and react badly. Yet all through Anne and Flannery's long hot winter they had risked ice kisses and snow melts out on the town's streets. Anne more than Flannery had proved willing to take chances in late courtyards or in underlit corners of paths; Flannery had fretted, at times, and Anne had kissed away her fears. But this day, Evergladed, it was Flannery whose hands were bolder. They started to move into areas that, in shorts, were easily accessed.

Anne gasped at her touch. "What are you doing?" she said in a shocked whisper, but the thrilled clutch of her nails against Flannery's back told her she knew perfectly well what Flannery was doing. And did not object.

"I want you," Flannery murmured, as if the want were not obvious. Her fingers found what they were looking for, and the two women became, temporarily, one.

Which was the shape they were found in by the young honeymooners who just then rounded the path.

"Oh my God" was the simultaneous exhalation of the two unhappy couples, who wished, too late, that they had not seen or been seen. *If only we had not looked.* If only we had not happened to be here—*now*.

What could anyone do? It was an impossible embarrassment all around.

Flannery did what she could: wrapped her arms entirely around Anne in an effort to hide her, then buried her own face in Anne's soft neck so she would not have to read the couple's expressions. It was she, Flannery, who faced them. Anne's back was to the pair, so all she had to go by was their sound of alarm and the sudden rigidity of Flannery's body.

"What the hell—?" the man said. He, of the two, was not inclined to stop looking.

"Come on, honey," said his mate, urging him on. Perhaps this was one of a series of efforts to lead him past his anger: Flannery opened her eyes just enough to see the woman's nervous, haunted eyes. "Let's go. Let's just go."

"What the hell do you think—"

"Come *on*." Desperation, or disgust, must have made her strong, as she succeeded in pulling the hulking man away. They moved into the woods in a tight alliance of stunned dismay, throwing back words that reached the two women's ears with a sting.

". . . Shameless . . . Did you see . . . ? . . . Indecent . . . *Freaks.*"

They stood clinging to each other on their sinking ship. The heat of intimacy gone, doused by the dampness of shamed humiliation and the thwarted violence that goes with it. Flannery found herself wanting to hit Anne, or bite her. The feeling was probably mutual.

It is an old story. One of the oldest. They would not have had to travel so far just to learn it: Lust—open, naked lust—must be named and punished. How else can we hope to keep the world in order?

Their conversation was dead, and a spring storm was coming. Clouds scowled overhead to remind them to get back to their car, as if they weren't going there already. Anything for self-protection, to cover themselves back up after the exposure of their sin.

They could neither look at nor speak to each other, which made it hard to work out how to proceed. Anne finally drove back into town, leaving Flannery at a diner where she could order grits. In the absence of Pop-Tarts, grits seemed the closest she would find to comfort food. Anne intended to drive around looking for a place for them to stay that night. They both could use some time on their own.

Flannery filled hers with reading. It was her time-tested response to crisis. She let Intro to Drama drive Florida and its demons out of her head. *I am not here*, she told herself calmly. *I am sitting near a bare tree, waiting for Godot*. "In spite of the tennis . . ." she mumbled aloud, after Lucky. "Tennis of all sorts." A pompous, acne-scarred boy in her class had pronounced the play "a boil on the face of literature," which was bound to make Flannery read it with even more sympathy. Hers was the kind of university where eighteen-year-olds were proud to issue such commentaries.

Flannery had to hope that she would not, in her four years, learn to speak similarly.

It was not easy to take herself out of the warm-voiced diner, full of group tables of sleepy tourists and solitary fish-skinned natives, and out into the spare-worded landscape of Beckett, but Flannery tried. She bummed a cigarette off a mascaraed, sun-leathered older woman with a wide swoop of an accent, and that somehow helped. By the time Anne came back, almost two hours later, Flannery was so deep in the text's elements and the comic despair of existence, that she was practically in Paris. *En attendant Godot*. Where she ought to have been now, anyway. Where this springtime, by rights, she belonged.

Anne came back to Flannery changed, and thwarted.

"Sorry I took so long. I had to make a couple of phone calls." She sat down, shifting in her clothes, as if they no longer fit her. She ordered a coffee. "Anyway. No luck on accommodation. It's the same problem as before: the motels have no vacancies, and the hotels are too damned expensive." She pulled out a cigarette and, seeing the butt in the ashtray, offered one to Flannery without comment. It seemed a peace offering. Flannery took it. Her mouth already had the taste of a crematorium.

"That's all right." Flannery had, in the course of her long wait, taken on an existential resignation. *Ça ne fait rien*. "No big deal."

"Do you want to drive farther? It might get less crowded if we head south."

"No. Let's not worry about it." Flannery nodded down at the book. "After all, we give birth astride a grave, so what's the difference?"

"Oh." Anne's eyes, seeing the cover, flickered to life. "Is that the first time you're reading it?"

"Of course." Flannery smoked with ridiculous, staged exuberance. "It's my first time for *everything*. First time in Florida—"

"Mine too."

"First time eating grits. Second, if you count Amtrak."

"Which I don't. I'm sure it was Cream of Wheat, trying to pass."

"First time"—Flannery lowered her voice—"getting caught having sex in a public place."

Anne winced. "Mine too."

"Really? With all your worldly experience?"

"With *all* my worldly experience. Believe it or not." But Anne was back now; back enough to talk to Flannery again. "You know, babe, there's an added plot twist here. A storm is coming."

"I know. I've been hearing all about it from the people in here." By now Flannery was unstoppably punchy. "But that's no surprise, is it?"

"What do you mean?"

"Well, obviously it's the wrath of God coming down on our heads. For our sin against nature."

"Oh." Anne's hard, perfect lips finally broke into the tiniest smile. Her brow lifted slightly. "You think?"

"Sure. Come on, sweetheart. Let's go watch." Flannery threw down a bill for her long breakfast and several coffees. "I bet you'll blush all over when it comes."

Parked at one edge of the world, they took in the performance. It was all about the elements, and in this way not so different from what Flannery had just been reading. A different cast, though. For Gogo and Didi Flannery read the troubled companionship of sky and water, with comic or painful relief provided by the wind brutally whipping the abject, mute trees. *In spite of the tennis.*

"It's not a hurricane," Anne clarified, to reassure them both. "It's the wrong season."

"So does it have a name? Don't they name them?"

"No, only hurricanes get names. And maybe tropical storms, too."

"*Murphy,*" Flannery suggested. " 'Tropical storm Murphy hit the Everglades today . . .'"

Anne looked out at the wet rage. "That Murphy," she said. "He is nothing but trouble. It was all his fault, if you remember. The shameful Park Incident."

"Absolutely. He was egging us on. 'Go, girls. I've got the cameras rolling. Go at it!'"

"Don't." Anne hid her eyes with her hands, though her voice still held some humor. "That huge man. Awful. Calling us *freaks.*" She kept her face hidden.

"He couldn't see that you were a woman, though. He wasn't sure. It was our being on the path that upset him. Fornication in public: he didn't like it."

"No, it wasn't just that. He knew we were two women. Why else would he say 'freaks'?"

"He wasn't sure," Flannery insisted. "He couldn't see you, or even me, really."

"I don't usually get mistaken for a man."

"I'm sure you don't. I don't, either. But when people don't know—it's not the first thing they guess."

"I think you're being naïve."

It was an odd thing to be arguing about. What difference did it make?

"We're not freaks," Flannery said. That was the main point. "We're just a couple of girls who got a little overexcited. We didn't mean to hurt anyone. We're nice girls, really."

Anne turned to watch Flannery. Poor pink Flannery. Anne brushed fond fingers through Flannery's sun-lightened hair—one of the few parts of her that did not hurt.

"You may be," Anne said gently, "a nice girl. I'm not."

Flannery leaned her head into Anne's hand, gratefully, like a cat inviting the caress. "Sure you are," she said. Around them the rain and wind drama continued, but it no longer had their full attention. "Sure you are. Ask Murphy. He agrees with me on this one."

"Oh, Flannery." Anne sighed, with the conviction of someone of a different generation. The cast of her voice made her seem older. Something about its new regret-hinting depth, its tenor of well-traveled tiredness. "I don't think so. I think Murphy knows otherwise."

Afternoon crept into evening, and they were still in the car. Talking.

The storm got them talking, and as it tantrumed on, the car became the calmest and most comfortable refuge in the world, warmed by their voices. Their new home's windows clouded with their condensed conversation, and the storm grew dark and night-blurred beyond them, a distant stampede outside.

Anne and Flannery spoke with a seriousness they had never attempted before about being two women in love. About what drew each of them toward a passion that was not the done thing: the kind that might or might not provoke the word "freaks." Anne knew all about how Flannery adored her, and Flannery had come to believe that Anne found her charming and cutely beautiful; but they had never, since the very first days, gone over the ground of being two women together. *Lesbians*, if that was what you cared to say about it. Anne had teased Flannery about going to the gay student group—she once said, "That's part of being an undergrad, babe: going to *meetings*"—but Flannery chose not to attend. She did not want to sit in a room with that labelous name; she was not ready for that yet. So far, she just wanted to shelter in Anne. She could worry about the rest later: the group talks and protests, the specialist bookstores and specialist books. She could read all about it later. As Anne was forever telling Flannery, she had plenty of time.

They talked about being women and not being men. They shared notes on their younger years: the joys of being a tomboy and the creeping dismay when you passed the age when that word still worked. They traded stories of early crushes (a tall, talkative librarian; the sexy girl on the swim team; a tough woman cop on some old TV show). Anne, unlike Flannery, had enjoyed a girlhood fumble with a friend in her father's pickup truck, a detail that had great vehicular romance for Flannery. They spoke of being—nominally—the same as each other, and the fallacy of assuming this meant deeper understanding or closeness than in the standard heterosexual arrangement. ("You, for one, are illegible to me half the time," Flannery admitted honestly, under the guise of banter. "I'm still working on my semiotics of Anne.") They acknowledged their situation's inherent unsafeties, and the mildness of their Everglade encounter compared to worse possibilities. Anne narrated a night when she had come home from a bar with a girlfriend and was chased the last two blocks by drunk men calling them *fucking dykes*.

Cautiously, Flannery voiced a few of her own untried thoughts on the matter. She mentioned her nascent curiosities about women, and also about men, and what either might have to do with the new and changing shape of her self. She and Anne talked some—sketchily, hesitantly; biography was still not Anne's forte— of mothers and fathers. Then: boyfriends. Flannery had little to say on that point beyond brief high-school stories, but Anne mentioned a man whom she had loved, deeply. A man she had spent a good deal of time with, a man who . . .

She paused. "One day I'll tell you all about it. Some other time." And as they were in the dark, Flannery could not see the rhythms that crossed Anne's face then. If she had, she would have asked to know more right away. She would not have waited. But there in the car, in the innocent dark, she took Anne's words at their invisible face value: one day, Anne promised, she would tell her all about it.

Night fell, but their talk warmed them. Outside, the noises slowed and the rage retreated; the wind gave up its fierce chase. Why look for a hotel now? They were parked on an out-of-the-way street, a deserted place from which they had watched the storm. Surely no one would bother them? They agreed easily—as easily as on anything yet on this trip—to spend the night in the car. Friends now, lovers, and also two women who could speak to and hold each other, Anne and Flannery slept finally, half-reclined, in the post-storm of quiet, at peace.

Till a 5-a.m. face appeared at the window, which woke Flannery into a fear so abrupt she was sure it had killed her.

It became a funny story later. So much does. The two came to tell the story slightly differently, but since by then they were apart, they never knew the other's version: where she paused for comic timing, how she earned the laugh. At least half of life's humiliations and indignities, Flannery discovered, turned out to be recyclable later into routines that made you good company. In fact, perhaps the entire endeavor was to lurch from one misadventure to another, collecting the raw material for stories: in an older, cynical phase, as Flannery grew into her writing self, she considered this brittle possibility. If it was so, then Florida had, after all, served her well. Even getting caught "wet-handed," the phrase Flannery coined for it, on a path in the Everglades, would one day make a good self-revealing joke.

They practiced it on each other on the train ride back. They survived a few more days of shrimp, beaches, and gators, but those first days were the ones that produced the stories.

" 'We were weaving on the road, Officer, and thought it would be safer to pull off. We didn't want to cause an accident,' " Anne intoned again in her politest sweetheart voice, half an octave or so above her speaking register (a full octave over her smoking seductress). This replay of that pre-dawn encounter took place in South Carolina, over vials of Gordon's gin Anne had smuggled back from the drinks car to her underage lover. It was late afternoon. The two women were sandy, unshowered, and plastered. They had returned the rental car with fifteen minutes to spare, to get back onto Amtrak.

"'Where are you two little ladies from?'" Drunk, Flannery finally let loose her most sprawling southern accent, which she had been desperate to try out for days now, ever since that nice buttery waitress in the bathroom of Shoney's. It was all Flannery could do, by the end of the trip, not to ask buffoonishly at a restaurant or diner, "Y'all have grits?" She had become a great grits connoisseur.

"'Little ladies,'" Anne repeated. "If only he knew."

"You were the little lady he was most interested in," Flannery said. "That's the only reason he didn't arrest us. He was dumbfounded by your beauty."

"Not at all. It was your virginal innocence that moved him."

"'We're just stray souls from a fancy university: look, Officer, here are our student IDs.' I can't believe we pulled that. It was shameless."

"It was more than shameless. It was *freakish* of us to pull the university card."

"Freakish!" Flannery nodded. "Now, see, *he* thought we were nice girls. The police officer. I told you we're nice girls. Or that we can at least pass."

"Sure we can *pass* as nice girls." Anne took a hit of Gordon's. "He very nearly killed you, Flannery. Even in the dark I could see you were blue with heart failure."

"I thought he was one of the panthers coming to wreak its revenge. I really did. I was still asleep. Plus his flashlight—it was so fucking bright, right in my face."

"You and that imaginary panther." Anne shook her head indulgently. "It wasn't a panther, babe. There are only about four of them left. It was a dog."

"It was a panther."

"It couldn't have been."

Flannery stole a slow, greedy look at her girlfriend. Jesus. Even ragged-edged with sleeplessness, even in the murk of an air-conditioned gin cloud, the woman was beautiful. Flannery would have kissed her, then and there, if she did not have the reprimand of the Everglades loud in her mind.

"Do you want me to pour gin all over your head?" she asked instead.

"Ooh, baby." Anne laughed. "I love it when you talk that way to me." She tilted Flannery's vial-threatening hand back from her. "But, since you ask—not especially."

"Then take my word for it. It was a silver panther. Dead, by the side of the road," Flannery said, then took a long swig of gin, like some old guy rocking on his porch, telling far-fetched stories from his wild, long-ago youth.

"You know that telephone call I made?"

Outside was rattling and black, Delaware or Maryland. They had more or less fallen off the train in D.C., made a failed effort to sober up, then retrained at Union Station for the last leg north. A few readers or all-night talkers hunched under the faint overhead lights as the train crossed back into Yankee territory. Flannery was passed out and drooling, unobtrusively, when Anne's serious voice reached her and staggered her back into consciousness.

"What?" She wiped her mouth of its sleep spit. One day Flannery would learn how to keep herself together, as Anne did.

"You know that call I made?" Anne repeated. "The day of the storm?"

"Oh. Yeah?" Flannery had no idea what Anne was talking about.

"It was UNM. I got the job."

"You got it?" Flannery sat up straighter. This was news. "That's great. Congratulations." She gave her a sloppy hug with stiffening, hungover limbs.

Anne seemed surprised by the embrace. "Thanks."

"Why didn't you tell me before?"

"I just wanted to think it over first. Quietly," she said. Quietly. "But also, you know—I thought you would be upset. I didn't want to spoil the trip."

So you acted like a witch for the first two days instead, Flannery was by now awake enough to think but not say aloud. Her sense of the chronology of those hot days was bleary. When had Anne known? Before or after the Everglades? When was the storm? Her brain was too gin-drowned and oxygen-starved for Flannery to work out the timing. Anyway, it didn't matter. Anne had the job now, that was the main thing.

"That's terrific, sweetheart. I'd toast you, but I can't possibly drink any more or I'll die." She gave her lover, instead, an affectionate ruffle of her head. It was an uncharacteristic gesture: Anne was not the sort of person whose coiffure you ruffled.

"Thank you, Flannery." But so formal and somber; as if accepting Flannery's condolences at a memorial service. Why should the newly employed be so sad already?

The real slide started then, and it happened fast. Everything was changing and being busily arranged, and Flannery—who at points that year had felt the first thrilling taste of being in control of her own life, and having a hand in its shaping—fell back into the familiar lull of passivity. Anne organized her final trip to Albuquerque a few weeks after their return; *final*, she kept calling it, *final*, as if it were an end and not a beginning. Her metabolism altered: she became more impatient and twitchy. She pleaded work as a reason to spend fewer nights together; she had a new load of papers to grade (was Flannery wrong to think she said that pointedly, as if to underline their difference in status?) and a crucial edit due soon on the near-done dissertation. Besides, she reminded Flannery in a teacherly way—were there not papers Flannery should be writing? Books she should be reading?

There certainly were. There were all manner of books Flannery had to make her own, intellectual territories she should conquer and colonize. She read a novel about the internment of Japanese Americans in the Second World War and was duly appalled. For her philosophy class, Mortal Questions, she thought about what it felt like to be a bat, along with other ponderables of consciousness, under Thomas Nagel's provocations. She avoided Physics for Poets, because although she wanted to be the kind of person who understood what quarks were, she was too intimidated actually to find out. And Intro to Drama was coming to an end with Caryl Churchill.

There was nothing for it but to read. Flannery read in early-morning dining halls and in her dusty, neglected dorm room, where she unearthed clothes she had forgotten she owned. As spring made the air kinder and everyone's eyes reopened at the possibility of warmth, Flannery even read outside again — on damp soft lawns and across benches, and sometimes, even, a few last sentences on her way in to class. As the days lengthened and the new light invited, Flannery kept her head down, and busied it loudly with page after page of printed words.

Spring! It's a time of renewal and rebirth. Buds and new growth, kittens and lambs. Isn't that right? If you live in a place where winter seriously damages and deprives you, drives you inside off the hard, iced streets—spring and its blossoms arrive to cheer you, coming over all feminine and nurturing. We are supposed to love it, to feel joyful. Warmed back to life. It's spring at last! Let the unfurling begin!

Flannery's affections were different from other people's; they always would be. She did not move in the seasonal step she was meant to. Many other students had also gone to Florida for their break and come back tan and healthy, while Flannery, after weeks of ugly peeling (skin rolling off whitely at the touch—"You're like a snake" was Anne's observation), had only a sallow ash to deepen her customary pallor. As the air lightened and people's dispositions grew sunnier, Flannery's heart contracted. She became Grinchlike. Sweet, benevolent Flannery might have kicked a lamb, if she'd seen one. Drowned a kitten. Even Susan Kim, over a Mortal Questions coffee, said, "You're looking a little lifeless these days. Is having a free will getting you down?"

She wished she could tell Susan: it was her lack of free will that was getting her down. It was her lover's determined determinism to close the door on her life here that had Flannery worried.

Mustn't it mean that Anne no longer loved her? Flannery could not get her to say anything so clear. Anne was perfectly pleasant to Flannery, and their nights, when they spent them together, were still raucous and racy. But fast—as if there weren't much time. Anne was on her way somewhere else. Flannery felt it happening, and tried to figure out how to fix it so that Anne would not leave her at the same time she left the university. How not to be the baby thrown out with that bathwater?

Anne, meanwhile, was collecting herself to go to Albuquerque again for a brief confirming visit. She was buttoning herself back up, packing her bags. There was no question (Flannery checked, just in case) of her wanting Flannery to come with her.

Anne was flying off, only for a few days. She would be back soon, she promised. In the meantime, Flannery could enjoy life here, among the bright T-shirts and new Frisbees of glorious spring.

Flannery felt the oncreep of death all around her, even as she waved at the others, fellow youths who had no idea what was coming. *Enjoy the Frisbee while you can*, her immensely old, grizzled self wanted to tell them. *It will all fade, faster than you know.*

Anne was gone. It was over. Their farewell had been both somber and perfunctory, and Flannery allowed herself the stagy, melodramatic conviction that she would never see her lover again. The night Anne left, Flannery slept in her dorm room as she often had of late, but this time its small cramped shape seemed overlarge and echoey, as if she herself had already moved out of it. She briefly considered wandering over to sleep in Anne's deserted, solitary apartment, far from the student fray, but rejected the desire as unhealthy and necrophiliac. "Necrophilia": a word she had learned from Anne, of course. Flannery could not remember how it had come up. Dracula? Gothic literature? Or perhaps the evil-flowered Baudelaire.

She was giving up, then. Was that it? And Flannery was willing to, too? Throw herself down on the grave, like a loyal dog, howling, till the cold finally claimed her and she could join her mistress in the great beyond?

The metaphor captured her attention for a moment. She tried to pursue it. Flannery had scarcely had a creative thought all year, at least since her neophyte love poem and a scattering of notes she had written in various degrees of lyricism for Anne. It was a pleasure to feel her mind work over imaginative territory again, even if this was a cliché. So was it her lover who was in the grave, or the love that had flourished between them? And what of this image of the loyal pooch following its mistress?

It gave her an idea.

That was a possibility. Flannery sat upright in an indigo-lit dorm bed. Wakened by the bright possibility suggested by her metaphor—and the sounds, out in the courtyard, of drunken carousers.

She would surprise her. That was it. She would surprise Anne. Flannery, bold, loyal soul that she was, would fly out to join her: there, exactly there, in the great beyond.

She watched herself perform the adult tricks of travel, all those calls she'd left up to Anne for their Florida trip: airline, car rental, airport limo. How would she pay for this extravagance? She'd think about that later, back home in the summer, when all she would have before her would be money worry and melancholy. For now, she just closed her eyes and charged it. It was as Nick once said to her when he bought tickets to see his favorite band play a gig in New York. When Flannery questioned his means, he said simply, "But, Flannery—that's why God created credit cards."

And how easy it was to leave this life, after all—this life that could feel so present and permanent that departing from it must seem to require a tear into a different dimension. There the bunch of them were, young hopefuls, decorating their annually purged dorm rooms with postcards and prints and favorite photographs of friends, filling them with hot pots and dried flowers, throw rugs and stereos. Houseplants, a lamp, maybe some furniture brought up by encouraging parents. They nested there like miniature grownups. As if this provisional student life—with its brushfire friendships and drink-addled intimacies, its gorging on knowledge and blind sexual indulgences—could possibly last. As if it were a home, of any kind at all: someplace to gather one's sense of self. Flannery had never felt for a minute that these months of shared living took place on anything other than quicksand, and it had given this whole year (these scant seven or eight months, into which an aging decade or so had been condensed) a sliding, wavery feel. She came from earthquake country and knew the dangers of building on landfill. That was, it seemed to Flannery, the best description of this willed group project of freshman year: construction on landfill. A collective confusion of impressions and tendencies, mostly castoffs with a few keepers. What was there to count on in any of it? What structure would remain, founded on that?

Susan Kim had become a real friend. Flannery felt it in her gut. The sharp, funny smoker had proved as good at Mortal Questions as she had been at Criticism, and always came up with an appealingly different angle. "Who do you *save?*" she asked early on when they encountered the utilitarian dilemma posed by the people starving on the lifeboat. "That's not the issue here. The point is, call your lawyer and talk about the boat company's liability. Get the class-action suit rolling. *Then* we'll talk about saving."

Flannery and Susan had talked about living together next year in their own apartment off-campus, "away from the rat pack." How much more human they could feel there. They would have great parties. And privacy. Flannery imagined shipping more of her books out here so it felt something like home. The two would cook, and talk at all hours, and one late night, Flannery might tell Susan, finally, the story of what had happened with Anne. *Remember those times you ran into us in the Yankee Doodle?*

She had thought Anne would be her anchor. She had thought—well, she hadn't spent a lot of time thinking, in truth, she had just loved, fallen, jumped—but she had come to think, or at least hope, that Anne might stay fast for her. Improbable though it was. That Anne might continue to be there: there, where Flannery wanted her.

She would not be, though. This much Flannery had understood: Anne would be somewhere else.

And Flannery had to find out, now, where that *else* was, and what was in it.

221

There was an abrupt surreality to leaving campus this way, while everyone else played and studied, making ready for another onslaught of finals. Flannery felt removed from the others, like an ill person heading off to hospital for a mysteriously serious operation, or an astronaut going on a mission into another atmosphere, leaving the earthlings behind in their mundane toil. (Some of which toil she had to take with her: Flannery wanted good grades as much as anyone.) Her impending departure gave the spring light a vividness as she walked around the campus, and made the old buildings now seem radiantly edged. She thought she must have a luminous difference about her, though she had told no one of her trip and it was unlikely that anyone would much notice her absence. Her roommate, Mary-Jo, had registered that Flannery often did not sleep in the dorm room, but she was far too discreet—or, more likely, indifferent—to ask her about it.

Feeling important, nervous, and possibly underpacked (she knew they had winters in New Mexico only because a high-school friend had gone skiing there; otherwise, the place was a blank to her), wondering which response her cinematic action would inspire—a soft-lit, romantic "It's you, babe," or comic revulsion: "What—you? Here? Why?"; eighteen years old and poised on that particular knife's edge between lucidity and blindness—Flannery got herself to the airport. She was ticketed and checked in, scanned and waved through, and she duly lounged, then boarded. Once she was inside the plane and strapping herself in, a calm settled over her as it became clear that she could not back out of this. Flannery Jansen, a quiet, writerly mouse from a one-horse town, was heading to New Mexico, for love. This would become part of her own story, however the narrative went on, ending or continuing: there would always be this episode in it. With Anne or without her, Flannery would make something of this adventure. *Did I ever tell you*, she would one night say to somebody, *about the time I flew to New Mexico, to see the woman I loved?*

As the plane took off, Flannery felt a surge of airborne optimism. It took her a moment to locate its source (other than the sheer rush of the pressure change). She was heading West. It was just that. The inarguable rightness of leaving East for West: always the better direction to travel in.

Gaining hope as the plane gained height, Flannery found herself leaving behind the lead-footed anxieties and realities that had fought with the swooping romance of this plan from the start. A low, taunting voice had ongoingly warned her: Anne has never seemed like someone who loves surprises. She likes to be aware of what's ahead of her. And she may, simply, not want you there. This scheme may backfire, in the worst way.

As they reached their cruising altitude, with the mortal world tinied beneath them, Flannery decided to believe otherwise. *Everything that rises must converge*, she reassured herself. It would be all right. Anne would be startled then excited to see her, won over by the sweet folly of Flannery flying to join her. Flannery would surprise her in the hotel lobby, they would go up to her hotel room . . . Here she lost a few minutes, her head turned to the small envelope of plane window, while coarse thoughts warmed her thighs and quickened her breathing. Yes, well. That part was bound to be fine. And *then*, you see, they could go out and celebrate. Of course! They could celebrate Anne's getting the job, and Flannery could prove how bighearted and open-armed she was, joyful for Anne about this opportunity, which would incidentally take her two thousand miles away.

Flannery felt punchy. This was not a heaviness, this trip. This was a lightness, a giddiness. She persuaded herself into the mood. Peanuts? the flight attendant offered. Sure! A cocktail? Why not? How about another? So the cocktails weren't complimentary, as a Coke would have been. So what? She was rich now—rich on credit. Borrowing beyond your means—that's what credit card companies loved you best for. They rewarded you handsomely, jacking up your limit, for performing precisely this kind of gallant, priceless gesture, which would send you spiraling into further debt. But she was not going to worry about that now. She was eighteen, for God's sake: an age when you're supposed to have some fun.

The flight attendant was nice enough, but succeeded in dissuading Flannery from a third drink. *You don't know the whole story, lady*, Flannery wanted to tell her. *This is the woman who sexually awakened me that we're talking about here. How could I not do this for her? How could I not fly out here, to keep her?*

By this time she was tipsy, as the plane itself seemed to be, as it juddered into its Albuquerque landing.

Flannery could not believe the ubiquity of tacos. They were practically the first thing she saw, a stall selling them, when she walked a bit unsteadily off the passageway into the tidy peach-and-teal interior of the Albuquerque airport. No, it wasn't an airport: it was a *Sunport*, with Native American symbols painted on its walls to prove it. The woman at the car rental desk, learning she was new to the state, asked Flannery if she knew the difference between red and green chiles. "A lot of visitors think the red's hotter, but it isn't: the green's hotter. Keep that in mind when you're ordering." Flannery thanked her for the information, and for the keys to the compact.

She loved the West.

She was foreign here, doubtless—why didn't she know Spanish? Why hadn't she been fed it since childhood, as any westerner should be?—but not so permanently foreign as she felt on the East Coast. This place she could learn; there were others here like her. She recognized as like her own the longer vowels and unsheltered faces. They walked slower, as she did. Flannery doubted she'd ever fit in in New York, or Massachusetts, or her blighted university state, which was supposed to be rural and beautiful in parts, a notion Flannery didn't for one minute believe. If Anne had been offered a place to teach in New York next year, it might have been different;

they would have been close, a train ride away, and Flannery might have had the continuing chance to follow that city in her lover's footsteps. Without Anne, Flannery couldn't imagine she would ever wear the changing air there as her own, or make the right jokes, or care about their baseball teams, or get the hang of the subway.

But the indifferent fact was that Flannery, Anneless, would learn New York anyway. Years later Flannery was to outgrow the need to wear sunglasses in New York City for her protection. She gazed up at the starry ceiling of Grand Central as at the face of an old friend, and it cast its astronomical light over her tolerantly. She finally learned which way was uptown and which downtown if she was walking in the Village along Broadway. (She would be a junior in college before she realized Wall Street was not uptown; after that, people's directions made much more sense to her.) One day—this is the kind of thing life turns up for a person—she might even walk those streets with another friend who was new to them and allow herself to perform, as if she were a drag artist, the ill-fitting role of guide to that city. She! *Flannery!* "This is New York City; these are its buildings and cafés; these are its famous corners; this is why."

Such lines are memorable, and we learn to repeat them.

People had affinities for places, as they did for one another. Flannery, for instance, had never shared a humor or rhythm with her western friend Cheryl, but she had with Susan and, yes, with Nick. Here, under this broad spring sun, Flannery knew she had arrived in a state she could live in. Albuquerque had sky light and land shapes—the ragged sobriety of the Sandia Mountains, the dun-colored bed of the mesa—that stirred her already, and she had not even left the lot of the Sunport.

What of Anne and her affinities? Flannery knew nothing of Anne's home. She considered the fact as she drove down the open, sun-spread road, breathing dry air through the rolled-down window. For once, she thought of Anne's silence as her own sadness rather than as a withholding that made Flannery feel greedy. ("Stop grabbing, for God's sake," Anne had said to her the first night in Florida, over an unpleasant dinner. Before they'd wrestled.) Anne had fled the place that had shaped her language and sensibility in ways Flannery would never know, unless she happened to go to Detroit to see for herself. And Anne did not wish to speak of it. That home stayed where she had left it—behind—and she had no intention of bringing it to life in stories or references. Flannery had asked what Anne would do if a teaching job came up in Michigan. "Ignore it," Anne told her. "I'd rather waitress." Love makes people narcissists: this, too, Flannery now saw. Anne's silence about where she came from was not to spite Flannery, which had been her self-centered conviction; it was to spite Detroit, for whatever insults and injuries it had inflicted on Anne's beautiful head.

So. New Mexico. What would black-jacketed Anne look like in this rugged place? The setting did not seem right for her, certainly not the way New York did. Oh, Flannery could imagine Anne venturing into the wilderness, driving to Santa Fe and Taos as the airline magazine had suggested, exploring pueblos and tiny churches and the great formations of rock and desert that would forever mimic the visions of Georgia O'Keeffe. Flannery remembered Anne's rich, dusty stories of her Mexican travels and knew that she could love it, this dry heat and stark beauty. But living here? That elegant figure driving by the strip malls Flannery kept passing en route to downtown? It was hard to picture. It was one of those narrative details that jarred, as if it should be edited out.

But as Flannery pulled into the hotel's lot, considering the improbability of Anne's landing here, she accepted this as another encounter with one of the world's fundamentals: that life patterns zigzag in randomness, when opportunities catch spark and personalities chance to connect. Often as not, a person's efforts to take the rationally chosen path are thwarted. An obvious New Yorker cannot find employment in New York and is removed to a different imaginative territory altogether, which offers other possibilities. On a Monday someone might read your job application, or request for clemency, or novel in verse—and the light would be right and the spirit optimistic, and you'd learn in a week that you were to be hired, or forgiven, or published. *Yes, you!* On a Tuesday the coffee would not taste as good, the weather was ominous, and the doors would close, gently but firmly: *Thank you for applying, but . . . We have considered your request, and regret that . . . A number of us very much enjoyed your work; however, in the end I'm afraid . . .* One geography vanishes, and with it an alternative future.

New Mexico. Here it was. And here was Flannery, in the place that had chosen Anne.

The problem with being young and making dramatic gestures—though the problem can also afflict dramatically gesturing older people—is that you may run into logistical difficulties that undercut the clean arc of your plan. The gears stick. The machinery clogs and stalls. If you manage it smoothly, your timing works perfectly, the encounter falls as it's meant to and has the upshot you're hoping for, and you do not have to spend, for example, several long hours in a canned-air-filled motel room, flipping impatiently from one cable channel to another, wondering when you will find Anne.

Somewhere in her optimistic head Flannery had perhaps figured that New Mexico would not just welcome westerner Flannery with open arms, but that it would announce to her, helpfully, how to locate her lover, so they could get going on their happy surprise reunion. Wouldn't it be obvious, from the Sunport, how Flannery was to find her?

It was not obvious. Flannery had arrived equipped with one piece of information—the name of Anne's hotel—but it was not enough to effect the rest. Flannery asked at the reception desk, her heartbeat a loud percussion to the question, whether Anne Arden was staying there. The answer was yes, but she was not there now, at two in the afternoon. An hour's waiting in the lobby made

Flannery wearier and sweatier, and eventually brought on the revelation that it would not be good to reunite in this state, when she was all wrinkled and travel worn. Unlike Anne, her prettiness was not the foolproof kind that could withstand dry air and tiredness without showing it. She needed to shower. Right. She should therefore—what? Rent her own room at the hotel? Wouldn't that be the suave thing?

Flannery asked about their rates. As nonchalant as she tried to be, even her extravagant self quailed at the figure. It was an impossible amount a night, half as much as the flight had been. For the privilege of a shower! She could not bring herself to pay it. A further hour into waiting, Flannery climbed back into her rental car and drove back toward the airport, having been told by a supercilious clerk that that was a likely place to find a cheaper room. (She had asked specifically for that—"someplace cheaper"—having not yet become versed in phrases like "a lower rate" or "a more economical option" and other polite euphemisms for a cash-strapped person's alternatives.)

Which was how she came to be in the El Dorado motel late that afternoon, where she showered in a narrow, thin-walled cabinet and then lay down, flipping between talk shows, music videos, and news to distract her from the new, slow drone of dread within her—and calling the hotel every half hour, trying to find Anne.

The hotel receptionist got tired of hearing from Flannery, and she did not hesitate to make that clear.

"I'm sorry, she hasn't come in yet," she said the fourth time Flannery called, her high note of service-job sorriness cracking to reveal the sour undertone of *What are you, some kind of stalker?* "Can I leave a message for her to call you?" She had asked this before. This time Flannery finally said, in an effort to enlist some sympathy, "No, see—it's a surprise. I want to surprise her. It's—it's her birthday," she added, on a whim.

"Oh," said the receptionist coolly. The birthday did not mollify her. Flannery thanked her, hung up, then swore at the woman's rudeness. The West might not, after all, be filled exclusively with the world's friendly and benign.

Eventually Flannery dozed. She was hungry, but wanted to wait to eat with Anne: that was part of the plan, part of the way it was supposed to work. At last, faint with growing doubt and hunger, she managed to get through to a different hotel receptionist, for whom the question of the whereabouts of Anne Arden was a new and interesting challenge.

"She's not in her room," the receptionist said. "But can you hold for a moment?" Flannery held, as a talking head on the television mutely narrated a litany of new wars and murders. "Miss?"

The voice came back cheerfully. "Yes, Ms. Arden is here at the hotel. She has a dinner reservation in the restaurant. Would you like me to tell her you're on the phone?"

"Oh! No. Thanks. No—thanks. I'll just meet her there. It's her birthday, you see— Thank you. Thanks—" Flannery staggered and stuttered. The receptionist, thanked more in five minutes than she would be for the rest of the evening, hung up to attend to other travelers' needs, while Flannery went into a small frenzy of anticipation in the worn, drab interior of her El Dorado.

Then again, why would she be?

Alone, that is.

Why would Anne be eating alone? Wouldn't it be stranger for her to be eating alone in the hotel restaurant, as if waiting for Flannery to arrive and fill the space across from her—as if Anne were the kind of person across from whom the space was ever likely to be empty? Flannery had hoped to find her there: an expectant, solitary figure, whose eyes would brighten at the surprise sight of her long-traveling lover. But wouldn't that, actually, have been stranger?

Of course she was not alone. She was having dinner with somebody, as Flannery immediately saw from the threshold of the restaurant, near the hostess's tidy podium, where before Flannery could ask for Anne Arden's table she saw the elegant tilt of Anne's tigery red head; that graceful neck; those gesturing, eloquent hands. Gesturing, in this instance, to the man she was with.

Flannery stopped, trapped in the dead time of the hostess's noon-bright "Table for one? Or will someone be joining you?" Flannery all but stalled out, checking her action, her impulsive move forward toward Anne. She almost tripped over her own surprise, so that the hostess's sun-smile briefly clouded. Wrong question, Flannery wanted to tell the hostess. The question is, Will

I be joining *her*? Does she want me to? "I'm just going to—hold on here," Flannery confided to the hostess, "for a second." She gripped the podium for support, as if she were considering making a speech.

This was no doubt one of the men hiring Anne, and she was trying to engage and attract him still, even though she had nailed the job. What did Flannery know of the mechanics of the world and its employments? Maybe Anne felt she had to seduce him—all of them—ongoingly. God knew she was good at it. Flannery watched Anne's technique from the podium. Here it came: her plans and ideas for courses she might teach, the finer dimensions of her dissertation's argument. A little flirtation. Why not? Anne did it without thinking, Flannery knew; it was a gift or a curse, something that came naturally along with her beauty: the insinu-ating eyes, the sly smile, the light touching of a sleeve or bare fore-arm as if to be friendly (and to note the possibility of being more than friendly). Flannery saw Anne touch the man's sleeve. She could not see Anne's face, but she could see his. It was animated, rugged with handsome features—a strong jaw, a long nose, a stern but humorous brow. He was looking at her not, Flannery noticed, with a new or nascent attraction. He watched her with something closer to slow, tender besottedness. Flannery looked back at Anne's hand on his sleeve. It was still there. Her fingers were play-ing, now, with the cuff of his shirt.

"I've just seen some friends of mine." Flannery felt she ought to keep the hostess up-to-date. Then she ambled over, casual Flannery, as if to say hello here to her two old, good friends. The besotted man saw her first and looked at her with a distant, toler-ant expression as if greeting a pretty but pestering student.

It was Anne who turned slowly, feeling a familiar breeze at her shoulder, but the surprise in her eyes when she found this known shape at her side was not the color Flannery had most fondly hoped for.

"Flannery!" Anne called out, a half-choke. And pale, glitter-eyed Anne, for the first time since Flannery had met her, actually blushed.

Flannery stood smiling and nodding, her hands tucked in the back pockets of her jeans, trapped safely away from where they wanted to be. She was underdressed, too: she saw now that Anne wore a beautiful silk shirt, one that Flannery did not recognize. Flannery could not speak just yet, but her nod was supposed to convey, Yep. That's right. It's me. I'm Flannery.

Anne let her face cool for a moment. Her smile was taut, the kind that might snap if you touched it. "How did you—?" She glanced at her dining companion. "What are you doing here?"

"Oh, you know," Flannery said in a high, offhand voice. She sounded younger when nervous. "I just thought I'd stop by." The line did not have the tone it had had in her inner ear all the times she had silently rehearsed it. It lacked the insouciance she had carefully planned.

"I can't—" Anne shook her head slightly, as if the act might cause Flannery to vanish. Her disbelief evidently carried with it distress, not pleasure. "I can't believe you're here."

"Would you—"

"Hi, I'm—"

The man and Flannery started to smooth over the awkwardness. Anne cut sharply through them both. "I'm sorry," she said. "Flannery, this is Jasper Elliot."

Flannery nodded again to agree—it seemed plausible enough—but her eyes asked for more.

"Jasper's an old—friend of mine. An old—"

Jasper drank some of his wine.

"And this"—Anne gestured with that hand, which touched Flannery's sleeve, too, and once there lingered fondly, unthinkingly—"this is Flannery Jansen." Then, finally catching Flannery's gray eyes, she added with a startled appreciation,

"My girlfriend."

Jasper Elliot did not say anything to that but "Pleased to meet you," with a salting of irony.

Introductions over, Anne hesitated. Flannery showed no intention of leaving or sitting down; she merely stood, sentrylike, as if ready to escort Anne away. Strapped by the lack of alternatives, Anne came up with a clear line of action.

"I'm in Room 303," she told Flannery. "I'll meet you up there in about half an hour."

And that was it. Flannery nodded again, amiably, then left them to their professorial chatter. Class was evidently dismissed.

They came together in a soulless cantaloupe-colored bedroom with prints of basket-weaving Indians on the walls. Lights from the pool outside gave the curtains an eerie chlorinated glow, while inside, a digital clock etched its rocket-red numbers into the darkness. Flannery had the urge to close her eyes to the unnatural light and southwestern kitsch, but then remembered something Anne had said to her on one of their first nights together: "Keep your eyes open, beautiful. You'll want to remember this."

She tried. She tried to keep them open now, but through open eyes she was bound to see what was in front of her: the woman she loved not altogether with her, here, though she was pretending and perhaps even attempting to be. Anne's movements seemed sincere enough, and her hands knew as well as ever where to go, but her own eyes were shut, as if in denial of what they were doing.

Their lovemaking was quick, more plot-driven than descriptive. It was not an evening for lyricism. Afterward, Flannery modestly pulled her jeans back on, then spent five long minutes in the bathroom alone, opening the faucet to cover the sound of her crying. She washed her face with water so hot it nearly burned her, so that her pale face was blotched with both heat and grief. She tried to comfort her skin with a hotel towel, but it was overstarched and scratchy, more enemy than friend. She looked into the fluorescently unkind mirror and it told her what she already suspected: *This is not one of your fairer nights.* She shrugged at the news. What do you expect?

Flannery went back into the room, ready with a lame joke about keeping up appearances, but there was no need to deliver it.

Anne was gone.

No note. No message.

A feeling rose in Flannery that she could not recognize. Whatever it was, Anne had never inspired it before.

Oh, yeah. *Rage*. That was it.

Flannery checked to see that Anne hadn't left altogether. Her briefcase was still there, a good sign. The obvious place to look was the hotel bar, so Flannery made her way there. (Would Jasper be there, too?) Shaking now with the thought that Anne was making Flannery chase after her. All these miles and months later, and this was still Flannery's role: to run like a pathetic puppy dog after Anne, panting eagerly for her mistress's attention. Why had that image ever appealed to her?

"*Fuck* this," she said out loud as she got lost and outraged in the maze of overbright corridors. "Fuck it."

Finally she found the lobby, and the Muzak, and the welcoming hostess, and the bar. Which harbored a despondent character in a clichéd slump over a shot glass, at one of the round tables on which was a colorful list of the eleven different margaritas the bar served. Anne looked so pitifully small there that Flannery's anger almost wavered. Almost.

Flannery sat down across from her, wordless, and Anne did

not even look up from her abject posture. The strategy, if it was one, was not going to draw Flannery back in.

It was so alien to Flannery—this distance from Anne. She had never known it so great before: not at college; not in Florida; and not even back home over Christmas, when, though they were thousands of miles apart, her every thought had been Anne-allotted. Even before Flannery had ever spoken to her, when she was still the loved and loathed Tuesday Anne, she felt more of an odd pulse of kinship, a convinced connection, than she did right now. Now she felt unmoored, unrelated. It was a strange, floating sensation.

"So," Flannery said, in a voice she could hardly hear as her own. "Now I know."

Anne did not lift her eyes.

"That's what sex feels like when it doesn't mean anything."

Anne winced at the remark, as if she'd been slapped. As she did, the waiter came up cautiously: he was experienced enough to know a bad scene when he was about to intrude on one.

"Ladies?" he said gently. "What can I get you? Another shot of tequila?" Anne nodded. "And—" He nodded toward the frowning young blonde. A pretty face, soured by sullenness.

"A White Russian for me."

Ordered more or less out of malice, as Flannery hadn't drunk one for months. But it had the desired effect. As soon as he'd gone, Anne brought her hand to her down-tilting face—as if those fine fingers would be able to hold back her tears.

Flannery sat at the table drinking, letting Anne cry. In Florida, at Shoney's, Flannery had cried in a public place, and now she was watching her lover do the same. It was all new. All of it. She was still learning something new, every single day. Still! What a testament to their inventive love's talent to educate.

Flannery craved a cigarette. Her nerves were so tense that only nicotine could soothe them, and for the first time, she genuinely understood how the drug worked. It wasn't just a prop or an affectation. It was a tool for mental health. She took one of Anne's from the pack on the table and lit up. Anne scarcely saw her.

By the time Flannery had smoked half of it, she was not so much soothed as completely dizzy. She had not eaten anything since the airplane's peanuts and Bloody Marys. Hunger, jetlag, and jealousy all filled her stomach with a bitter bile that threatened to rise to meet the tobacco clouds she was inhaling and the White Russian she was sipping. The drink was so sweet it made her mouth pucker. How had she ever enjoyed them?

Distracted by her sudden nausea, Flannery did not notice when Anne stopped crying. By the time Flannery stubbed out her cigarette—she thanked God it was finished, as it was killing her—she saw that Anne had pulled her face back together. Streaked but still elegant. With a careful index finger she made sure her eyeliner had not smeared, and even quickly reapplied her lipstick. A soft red shade Flannery had not seen before. Desert Deserter? Hot Tamale?

Flannery had never seen Anne cry. Not once. Through the haze of bad music and stomach rumbles she realized she had never seen those smooth cheeks tear-stained, or those green eyes reddened by salt.

They watched each other. No longer allies, as they had been, but not sure yet what else they might become.

"Darling," Anne said in a clear, resonant voice. "You shouldn't have come."

It was a tone of affection and regret rather than correction. Nevertheless, it put Flannery over the edge along which she had been nervously wavering. She excused herself rapidly to find a bathroom, where she could throw up all the incompatible juices that sluiced around inside her.

Darling. She had called Flannery *Darling.*

Flannery had never been Anne's darling, and the name made her break out in a cold chill of recognition that she was no longer Anne's babe.

As unpleasant as it was to retch in a hotel bathroom, and much as it reminded Flannery of those doomed bulimics back at college two thousand miles and several lifetimes away, her head felt a lot clearer afterward. She wasn't drunk, sick, or stupid. She knew who she was. She was Flannery. She had flown out to New Mexico to find out how her story went, and now that she was here, she might as well put herself out of any further suspense. It was time to find out.

She returned to the table.

"Are you all right?" Anne said, and though her softness of tone and outstretched hand threatened to bring on Flannery's own tears, she just nodded, bit her tongue, and sat down.

"It was a rocky flight," she said. "I feel better now."

"Look, I'm sorry. I didn't mean to put that so bluntly."

But of course she had. That was Anne: to be blunt. Flannery wouldn't have recognized her otherwise.

"It's so sweet of you to have come. And it's wonderful to see you—"

Flannery's skeptical look silenced the high note of fakery.

"It was a surprise, that's all. I didn't expect you, obviously."

"Obviously. Neither did Jasper, judging from his expression."

Anne didn't answer that.

"Why don't you tell me about him, Anne." It wasn't a question.

"What, now? God, Flannery—" She shook her head. "It's such a long story. You have no idea . . ."

"You're right. That's the problem. I don't." Flannery signaled to the waiter. She planned to order some food, and water. "Now," she said to Anne, her gray eyes as lucid as they had ever been. "For as long as it takes."

Jasper was, it turned out, Paris. He was Texas and Louisiana (though he was not Mexico: that was someone else). He was the man who played her Monk and the person who had given her that leather jacket, and a silk scarf she wore whenever she and Flannery ate somewhere "nice"; and also her treasured copy of *Les Fleurs du Mal*. He was a French historian. He was cultured and older, and he drank wine, of course. He spoke it fluently—French, as well as wine—and enough Italian to get by if they visited there (as they had), and though he was a timid driver, he was a keen walker and a good reader of maps. They had, over years, traveled, quarreled, near-married, weathered infidelities, then separated, when he got a professorship elsewhere and fell in love with someone else. That had been the previous summer. He was graceful, intelligent, musical; he played the clarinet, singingly. He had loved Anne's body with the confident tenderness of years, and had seen and felt it through changes of language and climate that domestic Flannery had not. He had kissed her endlessly and loved her thoroughly, but he had never found that place within Anne that Flannery had touched. He had not opened up his own body to her hands in the way that Flannery had. He had not drunk iced lemonade with her in coldest January, nor had he written any of his own words for her; the texts they shared were always other people's. And he did not know what it was like to be two women in love.

Some of these things Anne told Flannery. Some she figured out for herself.

What Flannery found hard to understand was why Anne had to break down again as she told her about Jasper. Flannery could not parse this crying.

"Why so sad, Anne?" she asked in a pause, after the kind waiter had brought her a restorative plate of cheese enchiladas. ("Would you like red or green chile sauce?" he had asked in a discreet, mortified whisper. Spice-lover, she chose green.) Once Flannery started eating, she felt better. If she could eat she was all right, and some survivalist instinct had returned her appetite to her for a short while. Through most of the rest of her short trip she would not be able to swallow a mouthful, and so would have to forgo New Mexico's other culinary treats.

"It's a nice story," Flannery said. "He's a great guy. You had fun together. Why the tears?"

Anne looked at her through grief-bloodied eyes. For once—literally for the first time since Flannery had caught sight of her, in the Yankee Doodle—Anne did not strike her as beautiful. Ah, because she was ashamed, that was why, and Flannery had never seen or remotely imagined her proud Anne ashamed.

"Why?" Anne repeated in disbelief. She could not hear Flannery's tone—whether it was bitterness or sarcasm, or blank, optimistic misapprehension.

"Yes." Flannery challenged her. "Why?"

The distance between them was by now immeasurable. Anne's expression suggested she had hardly met Flannery before. She shook her head.

"Because I still love him," Anne said, which Flannery had known and not known. Hearing Anne voice the words of her unspoken suspicion turned Flannery's last bite of food to lifeless ash in her mouth.

Flannery had always known his shape. Now she knew how he filled it. She had sensed the space around Anne where he had so recently been. It was palpable, no matter how close the two women had come. But now Flannery had textures to ascribe to the emptiness she had felt before: she knew the man's handsomeness and the quality of his voice; she knew the way his eyes drank Anne in as if he'd been wandering a thirsty desert for months. Flannery had no idea where he had gone after Anne had left the table to return to her room, but Flannery had to accept the fact that the hotel hummed, probably, with Jasper's presence still.

"What was he doing here? Did you plan to meet him?"

"No!" Anne said. Overemphatically. "No. I had no idea he'd come. But he teaches now at the University of Texas, in Austin, and it's not—that far. He must have heard they were planning to hire me. It's a small world; people talk. He knows the chair of the French Department here, at UNM."

She wondered if this was true. Did it matter? If Flannery was going to have to start listening for lies, not simply silences, didn't that mean it was already over?

"And what did he want? To say hi? Chew the fat? Reminisce?"

"Flannery—"

"No, really, what?" There was sharpness in Flannery, too. She would never have been drawn to Anne's edge in the first place if she did not have a hidden blade of her own. It was a self-truth Flannery had not yet accepted, one of the understandings she would come to later.

"He wants me back." The closing punctuation of "obviously" hung in the air. The confidence in her! Anne would always have it: the certainty that there would be a trail of people following her, wanting her love and her beauty. Flannery saw that confidence, and through the polluted air now between them it no longer charmed her. Not tonight it didn't. Flannery was not inclined to be one of that number. *I took the road less traveled by*, the romantic high-school students intoned to themselves when they read the famous Frost lines, which resonated with their wistful, independent selves. Flannery felt that way now. She would rather strike out on her own, far from the Anne-maddened crowd.

"I don't know what to do," Anne said. Her face pleaded—for time, or sympathy. Her voice was low and humble. But Flannery could not rule out the possibility, now, that the humility was staged. When had the conversation between them become so theatrical? In the last hour or two? Or had it happened earlier, when Flannery was not looking carefully?

"That's easy," Flannery said coolly, sipping the last of her ice water.

"Oh, it is?" Anne allowed some sarcasm to seep in.

"Sure." Flannery spread her hands, palms up, in front of her, an opening gesture. She leaned in toward Anne. "Take him."

And Flannery left the table, allowing her former lover to pick up the check.

Could it be that simple? Was that how these things ended? Did you just walk away, leave the room, pack your bag, and take the plane back to the city you had come from?

It turned out not to be that simple. Flannery wanted to match the drama of her flight out here with the drama of an immediate flight back, but she realized, after making a quick phone call, that it was too late to leave that night and the soonest she could return was late the following afternoon. Flannery had planned to stay two nights, the first, the happy surprise of reunion, and the second, calmer love after a day's exploration of New Mexican mesa or mountain, maybe even a fording of the Rio Grande. And now here she was, 11 p.m., 1 a.m. Eastern time, roomless and wandering, wondering which of the bad options before her to take. Find a room here at great expense, out of the fiery jealous conviction that she had to be in the same place as Anne to prevent *le beau* Jasper from reseizing her now, with the "Darling" all ready on his lips, and on hers? That, or she could crawl back to the El Dorado for a night of isolated misery. Or, even better—how low could these episodes go? how far down might someone like Flannery sink?—she could spend the night in her rental car, in the parking lot here, in nostalgic homage to the blighted state of Florida and a haunting fear of dead panthers.

"Flannery."

A hand on her elbow. She pulled away instinctively.

"What?" she said, not turning around from her blind progress down some random pastel corridor.

"What are you doing? Where are you going?"

The kindness in Anne's voice—the one Flannery knew about, that was hers—nearly broke her.

"I'm just—you know—I'm—"

Her shoulders slowly caved; she lost a couple of inches of her native height to sinking her face into her hands, hiding her own sudden tears from the woman who had caused them.

"Flannery," Anne said, holding her arms around her. How was it, now, that they were something like the same height? Had Anne recently grown? "Come with me."

And, unable to articulate anything dignified like *No, I can't*— Flannery did.

Such nights are possible, and we survive them.

It is a matter of sleeping next to the adored body you no longer have the right or inclination to love. Whether you are the one who casts off, or the castoff yourself; whether your arms are the recoilers, or the ones that reach wantingly, then pull back, remembering they are no longer wanted. Two bodies that are used to each other's rhythms and sleep sounds, that know the turnings and breathings, know not to worry about that cough or that brief garbled grunt, that wildly flung arm or that stone-cold foot. Bodies that soon will not know each other's night selves: will touch each other through jackets and jeans and the cooled-down air of re-established acquaintance, if such a thing is possible between a given pair of ex-lovers. When she was twenty, Flannery would meet up with Anne on the university campus, when Anne came back to visit: they'd hug, have lunch as they had planned to, and it would go awkwardly, leaving them both distressed and dissatisfied. When Flannery was twenty-one, Anne would, strangely, appear at Flannery's graduation, give her a tearful embrace, then vanish—only nodding at Flannery's proud mother, not allowing time even for an introduction. When Flannery was twenty-eight herself, she would run into Anne in New York, entirely by chance, on Prince Street in SoHo. The two women, older and more beautiful in their different ways (finally Flannery had discovered how to wear her hair; finally she was comfortable with the length of her gait), would throw their arms around each other as if they were long-lost sisters. Jasper would watch benignly, as would Flannery's smiling companion. A friend or a "friend"? It would not be clear.

Now they slept together. Flannery did sleep, though she had expected a night of itchy, blanched awakeness. Not a bit of it. Her mind curled up with its unhappy news like a potato bug balling itself into its hard gray shell: no light could come in there. Flannery slept long and still, the sleep of the dead, next to a restless and remorseful Anne, who had already, internally, made the decision Flannery had bid her to.

There had begun in Anne already, in the narrative Flannery later wistfully told herself, a slow, deep bleed of sadness. How could she willingly lose this glorious girl who had flown miles to see her, be with her, and love her? How could Anne release this Flannery freely back into her life and her future? With what fool-hardy abandon was Anne going to let Flannery continue on alone, to make her infinite ongoing discoveries in her own and other people's company?

Anne kissed her lover's shoulder with the tenderest lips so as not to wake her. Flannery wove the kiss into the texture of a dream. *People are cruel*, Anne had told her, *and they will do anything*, but surely that night she felt only kindness for her bright and brilliant Flannery.

There was time still for them to get through together. A whole day in the vast promise of New Mexico. What a foreign notion, that this could be a chore and not a gift for these two women, the striking, elusive redhead and the smart, sleepy-eyed blonde. *What a difference a day makes.* How true it was! This was another item about growing up: you encountered all the clichés of love and loss and heartbreak. During your own convinced moment, however long it lasted, you suddenly thought, Right. That was what they meant! Flannery wondered idly what other trite revelations awaited her. *Time heals all wounds:* was that one coming? And how old would she have to be before *Youth is wasted on the young* hit her with the gusting truth of a spring storm?

They could have separated, of course. Flannery offered her absence, a last selfless gift to Anne. In compensation for the surprise of her unwanted presence. "I can just peel off," she said. "I have a car, you don't have to babysit me."

"Oh, Flannery." Anne's back was to her as she sat on the hotel bed and changed into her top. She was still willing to change in the same room as Flannery, but seemed modest suddenly about showing her bare breasts. "Don't be silly. I couldn't let you do that. We'll just—wander around together. I'll show you the Old

Town. It's touristy mostly, but some of the old adobe buildings are wonderful."

"Think we'll see any gators?" It was a private little joke, a mournful nod to their botched spring in Florida, but Anne was all forward-looking now and did not catch it.

"Or we might have time to go to the petroglyphs—ancient carved markings, thousands of years old, on the rocks. I haven't seen those, and I'd like to."

"Fine." Flannery had next to no interest in stone carvings; it was a character flaw, no doubt. What was Anne now, a tour guide, planning sights and attractions for the two of them to visit? She had never seemed like a mother to Flannery, in spite of their charged teasing about it. But now she could hear Anne's suggestion as if in her mother's dear, affectionate voice. "*Petroglyphs*, honey. Don't they sound interesting?"

Flannery fumbled into her clothes from the night before. She had worn a shirt she knew Anne liked on her, though it was no longer clear whether or not Anne would notice it. As she dressed, a plaintive truth rang out in Flannery's head.

I never asked to go to any of these places with you. I wouldn't have cared if we had never gone anywhere. Yes—even Paris.

We could have traveled enough for me if we had just stayed in your room.

There were stores with soft-voiced white men selling Navajo blankets for vast sums of money; and small shops bright and weighty with silver and turquoise, staffed by long-haired women who might once have been hippies; and native New Mexicans seated against a long wall at the top of the square with jewelry displayed on the blankets before them. Flannery found the Old Town deeply depressing. The Ethnic and Labor History of the West: it was good that Flannery had been learning it, in small outrageous pieces, but how did knowing it help, when she was faced with such sights?

She was too gloomy to go along with Anne's forced light-hearted idea that they go try on cowboy hats or fringed suede vests. Shopping bored her. She had never before been bored in Anne's company. "Let's go," Flannery said. The whole exercise seemed pointless.

"Wait. I want to get you something." Anne steered them into a store with a theme: chiles.

Flannery was unable to hold back some sarcasm of her own. "What, you want to give me some salsa to take back as a souvenir? How special."

"No, no." Anne escorted Flannery to the back of the crammed store. There, amid garish red potholders and dish towels, fridge magnets and key rings, Anne found a small plastic packet and plucked it off the wall.

"Seeds?" Flannery was baffled. "Chile seeds?"

"Yes." Anne looked pleased. "Who knows? Maybe one day you'll be a gardener. You can plant them then. They'll last."

"I'll never be a gardener. I've murdered a couple of Mary-Jo's houseplants this year, though she was too nice to mind. My thumbs are black."

"I wouldn't say your thumbs are black. I would say your thumbs are . . ." Anne lowered her voice. "Artful."

"Don't say things like that to me anymore. It's not right." Flannery moved away from Anne over to the sticker section. Rolls of jalapeños awaited, ready to be peeled off to brighten or decorate. "I don't want any presents from you. There's nothing you can give me that will make this better."

Anne shrugged, but her eyes dimmed. "Fine. I'll get them for myself. I'll find a place with a garden when I move here."

It seemed to hurt Anne not to be able to make the gesture, but Flannery was past worrying about that. Anne put on her sunglasses as they returned to their cars for the last stop on this odd, melancholy itinerary. "I have already given you something, in any case," she said as they unlocked their parallel cars, "that you can't give me back."

"What? Your worldly wisdoms? A nodding acquaintance with Walter Benjamin?"

Anne shook her head. Stung enough now by the sharpness in her formerly sweet girlfriend that she seemed reluctant to finish the thought. But she carried on with a schooling face that brought to mind the old, brief teaching assistant—Tuesday Anne.

"You wait and see, Flannery," she said. "One day, when you least expect it, you'll use me. I'll be your muse."

But Anne might not have been as confident as she sounded. Her voice was loud, but only with bravado, and behind her shades her green eyes were red. In case it was not true, or was not a generous enough gift—to the woman who hoped, one day, to write—Anne intended to leave Flannery with something more material. She had always had deft fingers that could move cleverly. Up at the petroglyphs Anne found a way to slip the chile seeds unseen into Flannery's bag, where they would surprise Flannery later that night on the airplane, as she rummaged through her carry-on looking for butter-stained pages to read.

"I don't want to say goodbye at the cars," said Flannery.

"It's not—come on, now, it's not *goodbye*, as if we weren't going to see each other again. I'll be back in two days."

"I don't want to say goodbye at the cars," she repeated. Brave new demands surged through Flannery. Like a death-row prisoner, she felt confident that these late favors would be granted.

"What are the other options? Do you want me to come with you to the airport?"

"No. Don't do that." Flannery was emphatic. "It's not an airport, anyway, it's a Sunport."

"So what do you—"

"Here." Flannery stopped at a burnt red rock on which were sketched faint chalky lines, of symbols or figures. The petroglyphs required a certain amount of willed imagination to read. "Why not right here?"

"What—" Anne stopped, slightly breathless. Flannery had been walking so fast she was almost jogging. "What, we shake hands here, and then—what?"

"Just let me get back to my car and leave. You can check out a few more of those circles and arrows, up there." She pointed toward a high rock formation they had not yet reached. "There's nothing worse than people saying goodbye and then driving away in separate cars. I know, it's a western thing. There's nothing good about it."

Where did all this will come from, all of a sudden? How did the one who had never done any of this before know how to find the form for finishing? What Anne said was true, of course. This was not literally a last moment, or final frame. The mess of extrication was still to come. Ahead of them lay all those awkward sentences and hesitant requests, the broken dialogue that would unfold over the following weeks. *Do you still have my blue shirt?* And *I'm missing my copy of* Reflections *and need it for something I'm working on . . .* Worst of all: *Perhaps you had better give me back my keys.*

Before Anne had the chance to say that one, Flannery would send them back to her, tucked inside a copy of the unread Walter Benjamin. Addressed to Anne Arden, care of the Department of Comparative Literature. Via campus mail.

"So." Anne stood, wrong-footed. "What's your idea? We stand in the dust here and shake hands?"

But Flannery was altogether over Anne's wryness by now. She stood very tall on the rocky path. Straight, suddenly. Flannery had a grace in her height, if she could discover it. Maybe she was on her way, now, to discovering it.

In any case, she was no longer reading Anne for clues. Flannery was looking east across the Rio Grande and the flat expanse of Albuquerque to the grand Sandias. The fading sunlight sharpened their edges, rendering them severely magnificent.

"And so. Now—?" But Anne was arrested by the odd expression on Flannery's face.

"I saved your life," Flannery said, watching the mountainous light. "Remember telling me that?"

Anne almost smiled. "At that party? Sure I do." To Flannery's seriousness she said softly—as if not to wake a sleepwalker—"It was a joke. Remember?"

"You were falling, and I caught hold of you."

"Right," Anne said slowly. "But I wasn't in any real danger. I wasn't going to fall."

The light yawned between them, and time stretched itself elsewhere.

"All right," Anne said at last. To bring Flannery back, maybe, more than anything. Flannery did return briefly from the dusky solitude she had taken refuge in, back to those jade-worried eyes. She loved them still. Their Everglade green would color her vision for years. But Flannery was gone now, too. For her own self-protection, she had to make herself leave. *All right,* what? What had been the question?

"Thank you, Flannery," Anne said, her low voice a knife edge between sincerity and sarcasm, "for saving my life."

"You're welcome," Flannery replied, choosing to hear sincerity. Then she kissed Anne on those sweet lips and walked back down the steep, uneven path.

Wise and foolish. Whose bright idea was that paradox? It seemed unnecessarily taunting as a term for a person's second year into this educational adventure. If Anne and Flannery had still been together, they might have shared a knowing joke about the *sophomore slump*. Anne had occasionally made remarks, and not complimentary ones, about Flannery's posture. She had not realized Flannery's stoop was a self-effacement, an attempt to disguise her height.

Flannery was disguising it less now. She was inclined to keep her head up more of the time, to look at the sky and the light on her walk to campus from the chic, book-filled apartment she now shared with Susan Kim. (The chicness was all Susan's, but some of it wore off on Flannery.) Some mornings Flannery stopped off for breakfast at one of the half-dozen diners, Greek or American, that offered up their eggs and hash browns. One morning on a whim she bought a pack of Marlboros in a convenience store and then ate a cigarette-punctuated meal, just as she used to. The ash-flavored nostalgia soon struck her, however, as juvenile, if not foolish, and she thought it would be smarter, and wiser, not to try that stunt again. (Besides: she never had been convincing as a smoker.) Eighteen was too young, she told herself, to spend time looking back. She would have to get to the point—as she did—

when reading a thick book of theory over black coffee was her own act and not an imitation of Anne.

Over weeks Flannery came up with a long, looping route into campus that took her along one of the town's broad, tree-lined avenues, where she could watch the season's progressions toward its forthcoming splendor. The air began to bite and the temperature to drop, and Flannery felt her blood quicken with autumnal anticipation. October was always going to be the month for Flannery. Her new classes filled her with the promise of adventure; and her heart could hardly wait for the passionate hot fall of all those reds, yellows, and golds.

In that season, always, the words and the colors would go straight to her head.